Balancing the Scales

Balancing the Scales

by Laura Christian

ISBN: 979-8-9871415-2-6 (Paperback)
ISBN: 979-8-9871415-3-3 (E-book)

Cover design by GetCovers.com
Interior Book design by Laura Christian

Rambling Rhodesy Publishing
PO Box 3164
Sugar Land, TX 77486-3164

www.ramblingrhodesypublishing.com

First printing, 2023.

DEDICATION

For Jordan.

Without you, this book would never have been written.

I love you!

Chapter 1

Tiffin cringed as acrid smoke rolling off the valley below reached his nose. The fire had stopped burning three days ago, but the smoke lingered. Feeding his small herd of goats had taken the better part of his day since the fires had started, traveling nearly an hour each way to reach viable fields for his tiny herd to graze.

He tried not to grumble to himself as his horse lumbered by the ashen fields toward home. He wasn't the only one affected by the recent rash of blazes. Everyone was driving farther to feed their cattle, so what gave him the right to complain? The silver lining was that maybe his aunt would be home when he arrived.

Before the fires, he would feed the goats in the morning and spend the afternoons helping his father in the smithy. His first two choices for grazing fields were nothing but black soot coated in ash, and he had been traveling farther each day to viable grass. Sometimes now, she had returned from the castle before he got home, and she nearly always had a treat in hand.

Aunt Helen worked at the castle looking after Princess

Narette all day, making sure she had what she needed and did her lessons. His aunt had never had children of her own, but Tiffin had grown to think of her as his mother because she'd been raising him since before he could talk. It had taken some getting used to when she had been snatched up by the king's hand ten years ago, but he had come to realize that sharing her with the princess had its advantages.

Like the sweets. Tiffin loved the confections his aunt smuggled home each day. He couldn't imagine how they were produced, but the moment his tongue touched their surface, the "how" no longer mattered. He suspected someone in the kitchen was an etherae or had natural born ethereal powers.

Etherae were trained power users. Some were born with it, some learned it, but all trained at the Academy. Skill rankings were assigned by how many levels an individual could complete. Most trainees tapped out after the first few dozen and still became formidable assets to the kingdom.

Tiffin had always wanted to train, but his father, Aaron, had talked him out of this early on.

"Son, I know it looks like fun, but we have real work to do. Someone has to keep up with the thatch, someone has to look after the goats and horses, and you'd make a great blacksmith. You don't need powers or training for that."

The corners of his mouth turned down at the memory. Always with the responsibility. The last thing in the world he wanted to be was a blacksmith. It was an honest enough profession, but he watched his father day after day be abused and belittled by many of his customers, barely having time to eat, always covered in black powder and burns. If it wasn't for his aunt's constant scolding, he wouldn't sleep either.

Tiffin had never known his mother. She hadn't survived birthing him, so he had never had a chance to miss her. Some of the kids mocked him, but he had learned to let it go. They were also fighting for space to sleep, and Tiffin had no one besides his father and aunt to share space with. And being son to the town blacksmith did have some advantages.

His father was the strongest man Tiffin knew. He slung around slugs of iron like they were paper and was so tall, he nearly hit his head on the door frames as he came in and out of rooms. Tiffin regularly heard his friendly laugh as he talked to his customers, even the ugly ones. And his father's capacity for work seemed endless.

Best of all, Tiffin knew his father loved him. It was like a game between them. His father had a habit of randomly screaming Tiffin's name at the top of his lungs. When Tiffin jumped, nearly wetting his pants in shock sometimes, his father would glare at him before saying, "I love you." And then he would laugh and go about his business.

Tiffin swallowed back his complaints, grateful when the wind pushed the smoke's stench behind him. He inhaled the cleaner air deeply and picked up the pace. The goats bleated behind him, jumping around his horse, over each other, and generally having a lovely time.

The sun was just beginning its descent as he started down the hill toward the smithy shop attached to their home. Smoke billowed from the forge's stacks, black against the striking blue sky. The odor of smelt made his nose twitch. Even at this distance, he heard the steady clang of metal banging against hot metal. He hoped his father was making armor or a sword or something exciting, but it was probably just shoes for horses. That was where the bulk of his work came from. The king had commissioned him several times for special pieces, but mostly, horses needed shoes.

His horse, Gertrude, had not fully come to a stop before he jumped down and ran toward the door of their home. As anticipated, he found Aunt Helen inside, stirring a pot over the fire. Her head turned toward the door as he barreled through.

Tiffin wrapped his arms around her, hugging her tightly, which pointed out exactly how short she was getting standing next to him.

"Now don't go knocking me into the fire," she scolded gently as she hugged him back. "You might spill the stew."

Tiffin laughed, and he rolled his eyes with a smile as he squeezed her around the middle.

She kissed his forehead, grumbling as she did so. "If you keep getting bigger, I won't be able to kiss you anymore!"

"Then, it will be my turn," he teased.

At this, she pulled away. "You get much bigger, your dad will have you in the smithy apprenticing."

Frowning, Tiffin closed the door. "I know." He pouted. He had no choice in the matter, it seemed, growing like a proverbial weed as he was. Getting dressed every morning had become a game of how tight he could tolerate his clothing before the seams gave out.

If his aunt saw his unhappiness, she ignored it. She reached for their three bowls and set them on the table, placing a spoon beside each.

"Did you get those animals in their pens?" she asked.

When she didn't meet his eyes, it was clear that she already knew the answer. "We can't have those goats mucking about in the smithy, and you know they will, dumb creatures."

"No, ma'am." The goats should be his first priority, but after the long walk to and from the alternate pasture, they had to be tired. Tired goats caused less trouble.

"Go take care of that and wash yourself up. You smell like a horse." She wrinkled her nose. "And something worse." Her playful tone evaporated with the statement, and she stared at him with something akin to a scowl. "I want to talk about where you've been taking those animals to pasture over dinner."

Tiffin left to complete his chores and reached his horse first.

"Come on, Gertrude. You did well today, good girl."

He held the reins lightly, leading her to the stables and giving her a bucket of grain. To his good fortune, the goats had stayed nearby, and he ushered them to their pens easily. He made sure to latch the gate and address Gertrude's saddle before strolling through the back door of the smithy where his father kept a wash basin. He had filled the pitcher that morning and did not expect to see it untouched. He wondered if his father had skipped a midday meal again.

"Is that stew I smell?" his father's deep voice asked before iron reverberated against iron again.

Tiffin passed by the washing station to watch his father work. He always wondered how his father knew he was nearby. Leaning against an unoccupied workbench, he crossed his arms over his chest.

"Yes, sir. Aunt Helen told me to pen the goats and wash up."

Aaron swung the hammer down on the piece atop the anvil where he was working, and sparks flew. He glanced at Tiffin as his mammoth arm pulled the tool up into the air.

"If it was me, I wouldn't keep her waiting." Sparks flew again as the hammer dropped.

Tiffin moved to a safe distance to watch the great hammer fall again. "Your iron's getting cold."

His father frowned. "I know. Just a few more."

Studying the flat piece of metal, Tiffin wondered what it might become. "That's not a horseshoe," he pointed out.

His father's eyes crinkled over a half smile. "You're right. It's not."

"Are you going to tell me?"

"A hatchet." He heaved a deep breath. This time, he dropped the hammer neatly to the ground and wiped his brow with the back of his hand. "I'm ready for some stew."

"Have you eaten all day? Since breakfast?" Tiffin questioned.

"Of course I..." Aaron stopped wiping his fingers against his apron. His heavy brows knitted themselves together as his lips moved silently. "Huh. I guess I didn't." He reached behind his neck to pull off the apron.

Recognizing this gesture as an indication that he was definitely finished for the day, Tiffin scurried from his place. He knew his father would try to race him to the washing bin. If he lost, he'd be waiting while his father purposely dawdled, and then his aunt would come in scowling and berate them both for their immaturity.

Tiffin landed in front of the basin a split second quickly enough to win the battle and scooped out water sloppily, scrubbing his face. A scratchy cloth was pressed into his hands, and he wet it, stepping back to clean his face and ears. He scrubbed the back of his neck, the cool water soothing his warm skin.

His father dunked a second towel into the water, and they stood facing each other, letting the day's toils roll down their forearms onto the dirt floor. Everything between them had become a silly competition of late, and they compared who had the darkest rags when they were finished.

"Have the fields stopped burning yet?" his father asked.

Shrugging, Tiffin re-wet his rag. Soot swirled in the basin as he rinsed the dirt clear. He pulled it free and continued wiping down his arms.

"Mostly. They're still smoldering, so it's pretty smoky. Burns your eyes. I had to go all the way down by Gull's pass today," he explained.

His father frowned. "That's an awfully long way."

It was a long way, nearly triple the usual distance. But he took offense at the suggestion that he wasn't capable.

"Dad, I'm fourteen. I'm practically a man."

Aaron's lips twitched as he rubbed the dirt from between his fingers. "You're still my son, and there's a dragon on the loose."

"I haven't seen any dragons. Well, not the dangerous ones anyway. I've seen some evidence of the smaller ones. Maybe a belvine or a kreakcoon, but nothing to worry about. They're crop eaters, Dad."

"But the fields are on fire. It has to be a veseander or a

stiguine. And I'm hearing talk from my customers that it's the smoke making everyone sick."

He had heard the stories about the sickness spreading throughout the village, too. No one knew what started it, but everyone knew that it was always fatal. Bodies nearly melting from the fever. It wasn't like the consumption that started with a cough and ended with suffocation. This was something far more painful. His friend Gimble, who lived closer to town, said he'd heard neighbors crying in the night.

"I don't see how," Tiffin protested. "The forge is full of smoke, we cook our food over fire and smoke, and we're not getting sick."

"Just be careful," Aaron cautioned.

"I always am."

"I know. I know." His father's stern face softened as he wrung out his towel and draped it over a hook on the wall. "Come on. Let's not keep her waiting."

Tiffin finished up and trotted ahead of Aaron into the house.

"I brought Dad," he proclaimed as they passed through the door.

"You always have been good at herding the animals," his aunt teased, rocking in her chair near the fire. She had a pair of Tiffin's trousers in hand, patching a hole.

"Are you calling me an animal?" his father asked.

Aunt Helen arched a brow at him and shrugged. "Those words never left my lips."

He chuckled. "Uh, huh." He kissed the top of her head. "Welcome home, sis."

Tiffin watched his aunt lean affectionately into it before

she pushed him away. "Did you even try to clean up?"

His father shook his head. "Nope. Not even a little. Whatever's on the fire smells great."

Tiffin settled himself at the table. This was their usual banter. He knew a lot of other kids with siblings and adults with siblings, but very few of them loved each other the way his father and aunt loved each other. He wished for a sibling like that, but his father seemed either unable or unwilling to find a bride. Tiffin wasn't sure why he wasn't looking, but at this point, he was resigned to it. At least it was one less mouth to feed.

He choked down the stew, thinking it was a little thin, as the adults exchanged boring conversation that he tuned out until his aunt addressed him directly.

"So, tell me about these fields. I know you passed the fires because I smell them on you."

"Says he's all the way down by Gull's pass," his father answered, shoveling a large chunk of potato into his mouth. He huffed around it, chewing with his mouth open, as steam rolled out between his thick lips.

Aunt Helen cast a sidelong glance at Aaron. "I asked *him*. You've been in the smithy all day, and everything you know is hearsay. *He* smells like sulfur."

Tiffin drew back, sniffing his elbow. He hadn't been aware, but once he pressed his sleeve to his nostrils, the smell was overwhelming. He frowned. "I had to pass the first two places I usually go to find something fresh."

"Describe the fields you passed," she prompted.

Tiffin's forehead wrinkled as he contemplated her question. "They were...burned. And smoky. They look like coals that have nothing left to burn but can't stop trying."

She frowned, stirring her soup.

He watched her spoon going round and noticed with surprise that she'd barely eaten. Aunt Helen always had a clean plate. She didn't believe in wasting food. She folded her hands on the table and leaned in. "What about the ash? Is it on the ground? Or is it falling like snow?"

He thought about it. "I guess there was some floating around in the air, but we went around it. Didn't want to risk anything hot landing on the animals."

"Good. Smart. Don't go through it. The etherae held an assembly today. They think the sickness is spreading from the ash."

"If the field in Gull's Pass burns, it's going to be an overnight trip," Tiffin complained.

Both adults frowned, and he focused on his dinner.

Aaron set down his spoon, which got Tiffin's attention. "Tell us everything that happened at the assembly," his father prompted.

"Master Bastian addressed the court," she began. "He believes the same dragon has been terrorizing multiple kingdoms. Steward, Garlandia, and even Phoman have all suffered our same fate—fields burning, cattle starving, and people dying."

"And we're just now hearing about this?" Aaron questioned.

Helen held up a hand. "There is nothing we could have done, and you know the panic it would have caused if everyone had known. How do you prepare for a dragon attack?" she reasoned. With a sigh, she continued reporting.

"The attacks always start with the fields closest to the town, then a little farther out until the villages are practically empty just to feed their cattle. It's a pattern. First the nearest crops, then some farther out until the villages either died out or headed to other towns. After the second burning, the illness sets in. People burning with fever," Helen detailed. "And worse. The cure is practically a myth, and the sickness is fatal."

"Are we supposed to quarantine? Should I close the shop?" Aaron worried.

"No. That's not necessary," Helen assured. "They're gathering patients just to care for them together, but there's no evidence that it's spread by touch."

They paused, letting the information sink in.

"No one's ever heard of this before?" Aaron balked. "Dragons and dragon poison isn't new! Are we supposed to just lay down and die now?"

"Aaron," Aunt Helen soothed. "Calm yourself. This is not a personal attack. The etherae agree with you. They have been searching the ancient texts for healing methods."

"What are we supposed to do?" Tiffin worried.

"Don't get sick. Master Bastian talked a lot about how impossible the ingredients were to find for a long time. And then he said that even if they had the ingredients, it requires an etherae past the one hundredth level to make the cure. The one closest has been missing for weeks."

"People are missing?" Aaron reiterated.

"Yes. The best thing we can do is try not to be infected," she announced. "They're saying the ash from the burned fields is spreading the disease. We've all been cautioned to steer clear of it. Once you contract the sickness, it's fatal."

"Unless the etherae cure it," Tiffin interjected.

She nodded curtly. "Maybe. They were not hopeful. He had a lot of ifs. They have sent word to all the other grand masters, but by the time any of them could come to our aid, we could all be dead."

His father sighed, pushing his bowl away to lean on the table. "We'll figure something out. Just promise us you'll be cautious. I couldn't bear it if anything happened to you."

Tiffin met his father's hazel eyes. His gaze was unwavering and full of a sadness that Tiffin didn't understand.

"I promise," he swore.

He wasn't afraid of being away overnight. He had never done it before, though, and he couldn't help the inkling of doubt that crept into the back of his mind.

Aunt Helen sighed and patted his forearm. "Maybe you could take a swim in the river tomorrow. Maybe some fresh clothes as well. The staff washed your spares for me yesterday and told me how big you were getting."

Tiffin's cheeks warmed like someone had lit a fire on them, and he shifted uncomfortably in his seat. "Don't tell me that kinda stuff, Aunt Helen. I have to see them."

She leaped up from her seat and turned to the table beside the fireplace.

"I almost forgot," she announced. She turned back to them, carefully unfolding a cloth at the center of the table. Inside were two pink cookies, decorated with delicate lace-like frosting and what Tiffin thought for a moment were gold nuggets. "Narette didn't eat her sweets today, so she sent them home for us."

Tiffin and his father leaned over the table, so close that their noses nearly touched the confections they studied.

"Are these edible?" his father asked.

Aunt Helen's laugh filled the room. "As though I would bring you something that wasn't? Go. Eat. I had one at tea today. These are for you."

His father pulled away the top cookie to investigate, turning it over slowly. "I'll share with you," he offered.

She shook her head. "Please. Both of you. I know the stew was awful. It's not even stew anymore really. I tried to confiscate some left-over bones, but things are scarce in the kitchens. With the crops gone, this is the best I could do."

Tiffin nibbled the corner off one pale treat and hummed in delight. The texture was creamy beneath the crisp exterior. "Princess Narette gets the best sweets. Does she have her very own cook?"

"No, darling. Everyone in the royal family gets served these meals. Eat every last crumb. I didn't want them to go to waste. Plus, now that she's a bit older, I think she might be growing a little crush on you, Tiff. I think she's leaving them on purpose to share with you."

Tiffin's cheeks itched at her words. "Gross. No one likes me. I reek of horses. You tell me so all the time."

"And yet you do nothing to prevent the smell." She quirked an eyebrow and a grin in his direction. "No matter. Enjoy it till it's gone. And be careful when you're out, please."

"Yes, ma'am." Tiffin was excused from the table, and he carried the remainder of his treat to bed, to stare at the thatched roof and pick little bits of icing from the cookie and let them melt on his tongue as he contemplated the next day.

He hoped to have lessons at the castle again. He hadn't been there since the fires started, and he missed it. For years, Aunt Helen had sneaked him inside the castle, then he would tuck up under the long drapes around the walls of the princess's chambers and listen in to the lessons.

At first, he had hated the hours sitting still like a statue and didn't understand anything the tutors said. He often had to pinch himself awake during philosophy and Latin, but he had picked up more than he realized. The lessons about science and math were a different story. He found them particularly useful and soaked up every word, flaunting his knowledge over his father in the smithy as Aaron worked out special projects.

For the history lessons about the etherae, Tiffin hung on every word of every tale detailing what they were capable of and how their talents had been used to advance the kingdom over the ages. Etherae came in two varieties: natural born and trained. They were equally powerful, but natural-borns advanced more quickly in certain skills. A series of tests assessed every skill, and etherae were grouped into six levels, starting with apprentice. If he was gifted, it would take a year to complete his apprenticeship, but it was not uncommon for some apprenticeships to last up to three years. Most etherae peaked in the sixties. After level sixty, etherae were considered masters. If by some miracle, an etherae reached the one hundredth level, they were called grand masters.

Etherae lived by a creed that Tiffin had long since memorized. They agreed to use their powers to strengthen the kingdom and dedicated themselves to learning and practicing their arts to support the crown.

Tiffin liked to dream that he could be an etherae, riding dragons from kingdom to kingdom. He imagined herding cattle with them and chuckled softly at the prospect.

Tiffin had been saving the coins he earned shoeing horses for his father in hopes of being accepted at the etherae academy. The education might be free, but his food would not be, nor would the cost of the materials he'd need to study. But Tiffin was confident he would get there, no matter how many horses he had to shoe or cattle he had to care for in the meantime.

Chapter 2

The sun peeked out over the horizon the next morning as Tiffin led the goats to the nearest pasture. He gnawed at a hard roll—the last from the bin in the house. The animals skipped behind him, eager to get to the pasture. Beneath him, Gertrude responded to the goats, her gait prancing along with the goats.

He hummed a tune as they walked. It was still early, and mist swirled over the blackened fields. He squinted, relieved not to see any falling ash now. As he passed the second smoldering meadowland, his friend Gimble and his three cows joined them, headed in the same direction.

"Gimble," he greeted. "Morning."

The older boy waved, head low. "Morning." The word sounded grim on his lips.

Tiffin eyed him cautiously. Gimble was mostly good fun, but today, something was different. "Everything okay?"

The boy shrugged. "Fine. Fine as they can be when your brother gets called to the army, and you're still stuck here walking across the world just to find grass for some dumb cattle." He made a rude gesture at the cattle behind him.

Tiffin sighed. "I'm sorry, man. Next time, they'll call you. They call everyone eventually." He had been watching his neighbors as they were called, worried he might be called before he could begin etherae training. Maybe being away with the goats all day wasn't such a bad thing.

Gimble grumbled a string of soft curses that Tiffin almost didn't hear. "Not when you're the runt, they don't. Do you know what I would give to get off that farm and into the army? It has to be better than this."

"I don't call walking miles a day in that clanky armor better. Or easier. At least now you can take a nap under a shade tree while the cattle eat. No running or fighting or putting out dragon fires."

"Anything that puts me closer to Princess Narette is better than this." Gimble grinned, wagging his brows in Tiffin's direction.

Remembering his aunt's words from the day before, he suddenly felt a little protective of the princess. It was the polite thing to do when someone liked you. He shook his head at his friend.

"You could get put in the rank that digs trenches or latrines," he teased. "And you would never see more than a princess's turd."

Gimble groaned, making a rude gesture at Tiffin as they picked up the pace toward the pasture.

Thinking about the conversation with his family the night before, Tiffin glanced at his friend to let him in on the information.

"Hey, stay away from the burned fields," Tiffin cautioned. "My aunt told us that the royal etherae believe the ashes spread the sickness. None of your family have it, do they?" He dismounted, watching his friend follow suit.

"No." Gimble sighed gratefully. "But the neighbor's got it. I think Mrs. Thacker will pass any day now. Been screaming all night. You?"

"All clear for us. But Dad nearly never leaves the farm, and Aunt Helen's in the keep all day, so I think we're pretty safe. As long as I don't go frolicking in the ashes."

"Did you just say frolicking?" Gimble badgered, pretending to frolic ahead of his friend.

They took turns doing their best dances until they found their favorite shade tree alongside the grasslands, each leaning back against the rough bark to watch their animals chew grass.

Gimble relayed the entire affair of how his brother, barely a year older, had been recruited in excruciating detail and the glory of it all.

Tiffin listened as he slowly peeled away the bark from a twig, watching the clouds rolling overhead. They were thick and fluffy today, and he and Gimble took turns identifying interesting shapes as they drifted by. He looked up sharply as three of his goats stopped jumping, staring into nothing. Their ears twitched, and he swore at least one of them was trembling.

He sat up, swiftly alert as he watched them. The others were bleating, unaffected by whatever the concerned few had perceived. After a long minute of seeing nothing to concern him, he stopped checking the rest for similar reactions.

Tiffin leaned back against the tree as Gimble's cows lowed. In the same minute, Gimble sat up, scanning their surroundings.

"Do you see something?" Tiffin questioned.

"The cows do."

"The goats, too." He realized that a fourth goat was staring now.

They exchanged glances as they stood. Tiffin's eye caught as a shadow darkened the clouds overhead, and he pointed. "Is that..."

Gimble followed his gaze and squinted. "Why is it dark?"

The moment the answer came to Tiffin, he started racing for Gertrude. The hairs all over his neck and arms pricked to life.

"DRAGON!" he yelled.

The clouds burst apart overhead as a green, scaly dragon's head emerged, roaring loud enough to make blood run from Tiffin's ears. Cruel-looking horns lined ridges behind its eyes.

But none of that mattered. The gap between him and the dragon was closing fast. He could admire the creature another time.

He was already in motion, one leg not quite settled on Gertrude's back before they sprinted into the field. They circled the goats, pulling them into a small group before dashing away. He wanted to round up Gimble's cattle too, but his friend was merely a few gallops behind him, yelling the animal's names.

From the corner of his eye, Tiffin saw the large quadrupeds lumber into motion.

"Come on, you stupid beasts!" Gimble cried, spurring his horse near the creatures.

The cows scattered, two going toward Tiffin, the other heading the opposite direction.

There was a great blast of hot wind that nearly knocked him from his horse, and Tiffin gripped Gertrude's mane.

Gimble screamed.

The dragon was in freefall, barreling toward one of the cows. The green brute opened its maw wider than the forge. It leveled, mere feet from the ground without touching it, barreling forward faster than Gertrude could run.

There was a lightning flash of teeth clamping through the midsection of Gimble's cow. Its bovine face contorted into a scream, tongue lolling out much longer than seemed possible. Its eyes bugged out, and its rump thudded to the ground.

For a moment, Tiffin thought it was raining. Wet droplets pelted his head, running down his forehead and over his cheeks. He looked down at his forearms, covered in blood splatter, and realized it wasn't rain. It was guts and dragon spittle flying through the air. A plop of something pink and bloody landed on Gertrude's mane, and Tiffin would have vomited if he hadn't been so scared for their lives.

The dragon ascended in an instant as it tossed the front section of the cow in the air, catching it like a snack and soaring skyward. Tiffin goaded his horse faster, Gimble and the remaining cows barely keeping up. The goats screeched around him, and he hoped they didn't get trampled under Gertrude's pounding escape.

Despite the grim situation, he couldn't help but be amazed at the creature's coloration shimmering in the sky. The great wings stretched out in a span he was sure could cover his whole village. Leathery flesh beat against the air, taut under the strain. Its long neck writhed like a snake as the beast spiraled upward then wriggled as it circled. If Tiffin didn't know better, he'd have sworn the animal was cooing. The scales of its underbelly were very nearly white in contrast to the emerald of its face and body and they undulated all the way down to the tip of its spike-covered tail. He thought he saw a flash at the bottom of the creature's curved neck. It glinted against the pale belly, pulsing red and completely unnatural.

Tiffin's head snapped back to his getaway, and he focused all his attention on matching his ride to the horse beneath him, spurring her on faster, and continually glancing at his charges who were running along behind him as though their lives depended on it. Which they did.

Tiffin nearly fell off his mount as he gasped for breath several minutes later when he thought they were a safe distance to do so.

He turned to his friend, gasping out, "Are you okay? Are you hurt?"

The dragon's cry rumbled in the distance, and he could hear a terrible crunching noise and knew it was finishing off its fresh beef victuals. Tiffin's stomach roiled unhappily, and he squatted to catch his breath.

Tears painted clean streaks through the blood on Gimble's cheeks, and Tiffin pretended not to notice them. His friend dropped from his horse, resting his elbows on his knees, and panted for a minute before answering.

"My father's going to finish what that dragon started when he finds out we lost Trudy." He rubbed his forehead furiously and began pacing in circles.

"She's just a cow," Tiffin pointed out. "He should be more upset to lose you."

Gimble frowned. "Not everyone has a father like yours. He'll be more upset about the cow. He can make more kids. He has to buy cattle. Trudy was our best milking cow."

Tiffin matched his expression. "Tell him that your cow kept the dragon from scorching that whole field. He was hungry, and your cow distracted him."

"How can you know that?" Gimble griped. "It happened so fast. You yelled dragon, and the next thing I knew, Trudy was lunch. And he took her in two bites! TWO!" Gimble laid his head flat on his saddle, opening one eye to look down at Tiffin. "She was in so much pain."

Tiffin knew he was right. He'd suffered the terror in her cry and had pushed back his tears in his earnest desire to evade a similar fate. But it was over now and worrying about things in the past was a good way to get lost in a problem, his father had often admonished.

"Come on. Let's get home before it's dark. Are you okay to go on your own?"

Gimble mounted his horse and reached down a hand to Tiffin. "Yes. I'm good. Thank you for being a better shepherd than I was and saving the rest of us."

He waved off the compliment. "It was nothing. I'm glad I wasn't alone. Be safe."

Wasting no time, he climbed back on his mare and headed home at a healthy clip, debating whether to tell his father about what had happened. He certainly didn't plan to tell his aunt, or she'd tie him to her apron strings and drag him to the castle with her and never let him out of her sight. On second thought, maybe he should tell her.

He remembered he was supposed to have washed up in the river today at Aunt Helen's request. He considered turning toward the river, but he was terrified that the dragon would want more than Gimble's livestock, and he had ushered his entire group home as fast as their tiny legs were able to run after the terror of nearly being eaten. They rushed into their pen without fuss, curling up under the shade tree at its center.

When Tiffin entered the smithy to use the sink, a glowing red clump of iron landed on the dirt floor followed by tools, and his father kicked up dust as he rushed to Tiffin's side.

Aaron's hands clamped hard around Tiffin's upper arms, lifting him bodily and turning him around completely. Tiffin's feet landed toe to toe with his father, meeting Aaron's hazel eyes, exhaustion washing over him.

Enormous sooty hands roamed his face, lifted his chin, and tilted his head from side to side.

"What happened?" his father finally questioned.

Tiffin's eyes shut, and he dropped his chin, pulling gently away. "A dragon attacked the cattle."

His father was silent briefly, and Tiffin saw him looking out the open door to the goats who were merrily dancing in the pen, rested enough to be knocking each other down and nibbling at whatever they could find.

"There aren't any missing. I need more words."

"Gimble and his cows were sharing the field with us. We were watching the animals grazing, and the sky got dark, and then a dragon roared in. It was green. The biggest one I've ever seen. I've read about them, but they didn't describe how big it was." Tiffin stretched out his arms as far as he could reach and looked between them. "Enormous. Bigger than the house."

"I know what a dragon looks like, son. Tell me what happened," Aaron encouraged gently.

"It ate one of the cows." Tiffin remembered the blood rain and shivered. "Bit it right in half then played with it in flight."

His father crushed him to his chest, and Tiffin heard tiny sobs. He felt like he'd been clamped into a vice grip and wriggled.

"Dad, I'm fine," Tiffin protested, pushing at his father's chest. "And you're crushing me."

The arms locked around him released, and Tiffin eased back.

"You'd better go wash before your aunt sees you. We'll never hear the end of it." He passed Tiffin the pitcher and his towel off the hook near the basin. "Go to the well and wash right there. Just get it off your clothes and off your skin."

Nodding, Tiffin turned slowly toward the door, pitcher in one hand, rag in the other.

"You're okay? That's all cow blood?" Aaron waved a finger around him.

"And guts," Tiffin added. "But yes. I'm fine. Gertrude was fast, and we lost it. I think the dragon wanted the rest of the cow. I heard its bones breaking after we got away."

"Gimble wasn't hurt?" Aaron questioned.

Tiffin shook his head. "Afraid he's going to be in trouble. Like he could've foreseen a dragon attack."

Aaron's face contorted in appalled confusion. "I'm sorry for Gimble's family. They have the best milk cows."

Tiffin lifted a hand in agreement to placate his father. As he retreated, he heard the sound of iron tinging against iron again, and the normalcy of it soothed his overwhelmed brain.

Everything was ordinary. Nothing was amiss. Just another day of herding livestock.

He dropped the pitcher and rag near the house, ignoring his father's directions. Gertrude was standing near the goats, and he grabbed her reins as he walked to the river instead. Washing at the well would take hours. He needed all the goo out of his clothes. It was beginning to dry.

The cool waters rushed past his hips as he waded into the river. Gertrude followed him in, and he spent a good amount of time washing the chunks out of her mane. She barely even resisted. When she had had enough, she trotted up on the shore, munching on the delicate growth near the banks.

He scrubbed the gore from his head first, then his cheeks, and worked his way over his body. He thought he might rub his fingernails completely off as he picked the remains of the beast from his sleeves and hair. As soon as he thought he'd gotten it all, he'd find another lump lodged behind his ear or at the nape of his neck.

It was hard to think about much when he was in the river. When his brain was too full like it was now, water gushing around tiny rocks and rushing through plants stubbornly trying to encroach on the edges made such a racket it tuned out everything else. If it wasn't for the distraction, he'd be thinking that cow innards were the worst thing he'd ever smell. Between the blood, flesh, and intestines, he wasn't sure which was the worst.

When he had gotten as much off as he could find, he hauled himself onto a large rock near the edge and waited while the water dripped off him and rolled back to its source. He used a twig to scrape out what was left from under his nails while the rest of him dried.

His mind went back to the dragon, mentally cataloging all its features. Its head had been ridged with horns the size of his fist running in neat rows down each peak. Its pupils were slits over purple irises. Its mouth boasted dozens of teeth, cruelly sharp, and he imagined the cow's flesh rending between them as they snapped together.

For someone unschooled, Tiffin considered that he knew a lot about dragons. There were five basic types: grinkolese, kreakcoon, belvine, stiguine, and veseander, as well as subtle variations of each. He knew which ones were the largest, which were the most dangerous, and which ones ate the most. Some were carnivores, some herbivores.

The dragon that ate Trudy had been a stiguine. He could tell by the shape of its head, the spikes on its tail, and its smooth underbelly. He congratulated himself on not only recognizing the threat first but also the dragon type.

Gimble had been lucky the dragon had been satisfied with the single cow. Stiguine were known for their incredible hunger, although they were not insatiable. They were among the largest of the dragons, requiring the most food to sustain themselves, especially in flight. While among the most dangerous beasts, they were not easily provoked. It was far more likely to be attacked by a veseander or a grinkolese than a stiguine.

He wondered at the red, pulsing object he'd seen on the creature's neck. In all the stories he'd heard and drawings he'd seen, none of them had ever had something like that. The whole beast was comprised entirely of shades of green. The red was completely out of place. He tried to remember more details, but it had been high above him when he'd noticed it, and the minutiae was a bit fuzzy.

His aunt's story about the etherae's warning flooded back. They were right. This dragon was known for its poisonous fire, which would create equally poisonous ash.

Tiffin frowned at the thought. Stiguines were only dangerous when provoked. Or hungry. But as gruesome as it had been to watch it devour Trudy, the dragon hadn't been malicious. It hadn't even made a puff of smoke. Stiguine attacks looked like concentrated blasts of fire no more than three to four feet in diameter. Why would it burn large swaths of fields for no reason at all?

And if the stiguine had been attacked near one of the burned-out fields, how would anyone have accomplished it? Stiguines were generally high in the sky, blending in because of their pale bellies. Someone would have to go to great lengths to provoke something they couldn't see.

Tiffin stared upward, searching for shadows of the beast, but all he saw were puffy clouds and blue skies.

Chapter 3

By the time he'd dried and walked home with Gertrude, Tiffin's belly was rumbling. Aunt Helen usually picked up supplies about this time of the week, and he was dreaming of a sizable chunk of bread, and maybe some cheese she'd put up that spring.

He was surprised to find no smoke coming from the chimney. The rhythmic clinking of his father working iron punctuated his steps, and he pushed the door open gently.

"Aunt Helen? Are you here?" he called.

There was no answer. She was nowhere to be found, so he built up the fire in the fireplace then wandered back to his father's workshop, standing at a far enough distance as to be safe.

"Dad, did Aunt Helen say she was staying at the castle tonight?"

The clanging stopped as his father looked up from his work. "No. Isn't she in the house?"

Tiffin shook his head. "I looked. I got the fire going. Maybe she's caught up with the princess."

His father sniffed the air, then scowled, wiping his hands on his apron and setting down his tools.

"I've been so busy today, I haven't looked," he confessed.

The pair walked to the house together, finding the small

fire Tiffin had started roaring gently, but the house was otherwise empty. It was getting late for her to still be away.

"Should I go to the castle to find her?" Tiffin asked.

His father frowned for a minute, taking a deep breath and releasing it slowly. "No. Best to go in the morning. At this hour, she shouldn't be traveling the roads, and neither should we. She's probably staying with the princess, or maybe the etherae have closed the gates. We'll go at first light and check on her. I don't want to get her in trouble."

Tiffin enjoyed the privilege they gained through his aunt's ties to the castle. And if he was honest, he liked watching the princess during her studies. Her hair was the color of her favorite honey cakes, and it looked soft. She had a nice dimple on her left cheek when she smiled after correctly answering her tutor's queries. He didn't understand where dimples came from, or how one acquired one, but the topic had been occupying an increasingly significant portion of his thoughts.

His father broke out a slab of cheese for them both and split what was left of the vegetables from under the house. They went to bed early after they ate, but neither slept much.

As the sun crested the horizon, Tiffin was nearly one foot out the door when his father caught him.

"Where are you going?"

"Castle. Make sure Aunt Helen's okay."

He nodded. "I'm going with you."

Tiffin froze. His father almost never came to the castle. Even when he did business for the king, the king's messenger came to the smithy.

"You never go there. You say it's not you-sized."

"It's your aunt. I don't matter in this." Aaron combed his thick fingers through his unruly hair. "I'm worried."

That statement frightened Tiffin. His father mostly worked and slept and ate, but when he had a *feeling*...he was nearly always right. On a normal day, he'd already be at the forge, feeding the fires and preparing for the day's work. The fact that he was not was all the proof Tiffin needed that something was seriously wrong. He swallowed back his fear, then straightened up and looked to his father for direction.

"Get both horses," he instructed. "I'm gathering some supplies. I'll meet you in the stables."

"Supplies? We're going up to the castle."

His father's stern look pushed him out the door. He had the horses ready in no time and awaited his father atop Gertrude.

Aaron ducked out the front door with a satchel slung around his shoulders. His father was a large man, and Tiffin noted it often, but it was never quite so prominent as when he stood next to a horse.

Aaron swung himself easily into the saddle, and they started off at a brisk pace.

Tiffin sprinted forward as they approached the castle gates and passed through without hassle. He recognized one of the guards and waved politely as they passed. The guards made no motion to stop them, and he again thought how good it was to be known.

"This way, Dad."

He slowed his pace, weaving around the smaller streets leading directly to the kitchens. They tied their horses to a hitching post near the door and ventured inside.

"Tiffin!" a husky voice called out amidst the steaming chaos of a dozen people racing back and forth with dishes and pots and pans. Maids were coming in and out, rushing out with trays of beautiful food.

He turned to the familiar voice with a smile. "Myra. Good morning."

"What are you doing here so early?" she asked pleasantly. "Did you grow since I last saw you? It's been over a week. Where have you been?"

Tiffin was about to be drawn into the usual conversation, but he sensed his father's presence behind him. "Herding goats. I'm looking for my aunt," he blurted.

"Oh, I haven't seen her today. Are you sure she's here?

It's awfully early. Have you eaten? You look skinny," she complained. "Here." She pressed a warm, fat roll into his hand. She looked past him to his father. "Who's this?" she asked, eyes narrowing.

"This is my dad," he answered, tearing the soft roll in half and passing a piece to his father.

He refused.

Myra wagged a finger. "I gave that to you," she scolded. Like a whirlwind, she spun and held two large rolls aloft for his father. "Have your own. You look like you could use it." She winked at him, then wiped her hands clean on her apron. "And does Dad have a name?"

"Aaron," his father answered gently.

"Myra," the cook replied with a hand to her ample chest.

Aaron looked down at her gravely. "Could you point us in the direction of my sister? She didn't come home last night, and that's unlike her."

The woman's brows thatched, her mouth forming a moue of concern. "Haven't seen her. But she could be anywhere. I'd start in the courtyard if I was you. But be quick about it. You know the rules," she added, turning her scrutiny on Tiffin.

"Yes, ma'am," he replied. Tiffin could travel anywhere he wanted as long as he wasn't seen.

"I do hope you find her," Myra offered. "Helen's everyone's favorite."

"Ours too," his father replied.

With a brief thanks, they backed away, and Tiffin led them toward the courtyard.

He shoved half his roll into his mouth as he walked. It wasn't uncommon for Tiffin to be roaming the grounds with a roll in hand. This was one of the sweet ones. His favorite. He kept his head down, but his eyes scanned the area, pressing as close to the walls as he dared without drawing attention.

As he watched his father attempting to skulk behind him, he realized again exactly how oversized he was, and Tiffin had a moment of sympathy. It was impossible for him not to garner attention. His father had never looked more like a lumbering oak tree than he did now.

"You know your way around here pretty well," his father mumbled.

Tiffin nodded. "I've been coming here forever. I do pay attention, Dad." He walked a little faster, easily navigating the maze of pathways until they finally reached the princess's favorite yard.

The princess was two years older than Tiffin, but she was about four inches shorter. He saw her now prone on her favorite bench beneath a dogwood tree, silky, golden hair spilling over her arms where she had buried her head. He had seen her bored, happy, angry, silly, but he had never seen her crying before. He didn't like it one bit, and he hurried to her side.

The guards nearby tensed as he approached, and he stopped about a foot away, dropping to his knees.

"Narette," he murmured. "What's wrong?"

Her pale hair stuck to her tear-covered cheeks, and she lunged toward him. Her arms looped around his neck and squeezed tightly.

"Tiffin," she cried.

Shocked, he wrapped his arms around her, eyeing the guards that had moved closer. He held his palms toward them to indicate that he meant no harm. "What happened?"

"It's Helen," she sobbed.

Tiffin pulled away suddenly, leaning down until he could stare into her eyes. He realized how unusual it was for the princess to be alone. Helen was like her shadow.

"What about my aunt?"

"She's got the sickness," Princess Narette croaked. "It started last night. She was combing my hair and then there was blood, and she fell over. Her eyes, Tiff. They were...they were bleeding."

At this, Tiffin's balance shifted, and he landed on his behind, staring at her. "Where is she?" he demanded.

Aaron appeared behind him, lifting him to his feet and backing away from the princess.

The guards moved closer, their armor clinking.

"Stop. It's Tiffin," the princess yelled, hand in the air. She whirled on them. "Are you completely unaware of what's going on?" She didn't wait for an answer, her eyes assessing Aaron. "Is this your father?"

Tiffin nodded.

Narette reached for Tiffin's hand and tugged him along behind her as she ran to the guards. Her chin jutted defiantly up as she stopped inches short of running into them. "These are Helen's kin. Take them to her. Do not make me tell you twice," she threatened.

Tiffin stumbled along behind her. His father followed easily.

"Thank you," his father murmured.

The princess inclined her head to them both then turned back to the courtyard.

Tiffin followed the guards tasked with taking them to his aunt through a series of hallways he had never seen until they finally stopped at a door. He was coming out of his skin, looking up at the familiar guards expectantly and wondering why they hadn't spoken.

One guard looked between him and his father. His voice was soft, his words chosen slowly. "Understand that Helen is a cherished member of the royal family. Our highest ranking etherae have been tending her since it began. We are doing everything we can."

He pushed the door open gently, standing outside to allow them entry.

Tiffin didn't wait for further invitation before he burst through the passageway and stopped a few steps in.

The room was moderately sized with its own fireplace on one wall. A small bed was positioned near it with a chair on one side.

Helen lay prone in the center of the bed, still, eyes closed, and face pale. She was covered to the armpits with a crisp white sheet and a brocade blanket nearly the color of blood. Her dark hair splayed around her face and over her shoulders, a clump stuck to one damp cheek. The firelight danced over her gray skin. She looked gaunt. He rushed to her side, kneeling and taking her hand.

"Aunt Helen?" he prompted.

She was motionless, but he could hear her breathing, labored and shallow. Aunt Helen had always been a terrible sleeper, and he couldn't turn over in bed across the house without waking her. He squeezed her hand tighter and tighter, waiting for her to spring to life.

His father shuffled to the other side of the bed, sitting on the edge, and taking her other hand between both of his.

"Sis," he murmured gently. "Helen, please."

At first, she gave no indication of having heard him. Then, she stirred with a sharp inhale. Her eyes fluttered open, and her jaw clenched. She almost hid the groan that escaped her throat.

"Aaron..." she crooned, her usually bright voice a ghost of itself. Her head turned sluggishly until Tiffin could see her eyes, tiny lines of blood running throughout. "Tiffin." She offered him a weak smile.

"We got worried when you didn't come home last night," he announced.

"And it seems our concern was well founded," Aaron added.

Her smile was beginning to fade, and her eyes shut for a moment. A faint whistle escaped her lips with each breath.

"She needs to rest," commanded an unfamiliar voice behind him.

Tiffin looked over his shoulder to see a new face in the doorway. He didn't recognize the man.

"Come with me," the stranger instructed.

Tiffin and his father hesitated, but then Aaron stood, leaning down to kiss Helen's forehead. "We love you. Hang in there. We'll get through this."

Tiffin saw the tear that disappeared into his father's beard as the stranger led the way out.

Another series of corridors followed, and they entered another room and closed the door. One guard remained inside, the other outside.

The man's hands clasped together beneath the long, bell sleeves of his gold robes. Tiffin recognized them instantly as the garb of a high-ranking master level etherae.

"What happened to my sister?" his father demanded, hands poised on his hips. He was standing at his full height now, his shadow towering over the man they had followed.

"She has the sickness." The statement was profound in its simplicity. His expression was grim as he spoke again. "I feel I must prepare you. There have been many cases...none have survived."

Tiffin heard his father's gasp. His own mind reeled, remembering Gimble's words about his neighbor's screaming. If what he had heard was true, it meant she was dying. And it would be a long, painful process. His eyes stung at the thought, and he fought to remain clear headed.

Aaron's shoulders sagged, and he shook his head. "How did this happen? She said the etherae had warned everyone to stay away from the fields, but she never goes anywhere near the pastures. She's always here."

"I am aware. I gave the warning to the entire castle two days ago." He folded his hands in front of himself, staring into Aaron's accusatory gaze.

Tiffin stared at the man while Aaron lobbed question after question about how the castle had allowed this to happen.

Wisps of gray hair circled the etherae's head like a halo. His exposed scalp was freckled with liver spots, and the skin sagged in rings beneath his hair. He had the beginnings of jowls, which Tiffin predicted would have been enormous if the man wasn't also skin and bones. And, most important, he was withholding information; Tiffin was sure of it.

"It was a stiguine dragon that burned the fields, wasn't it?" Tiffin interrupted.

The etherae met his gaze and dipped his head in assent. "Very astute. How did you guess?"

"He attacked my friend and me while we had cattle in the pasture. Tore a cow in two in one bite."

The man grabbed Tiffin's arm. "You survived?"

Tiffin didn't like being grabbed and pulled himself free. "Clearly." He brushed his sleeve straight.

"Yes, yes, of course," the etherae mused, worrying his hands close to his chest. His gray eyes studied Tiffin eerily, from his face to his hands to his legs.

"Have you had any ill humors? Hot like the fire? Coughing?"

Tiffin shook his head. "Fine."

"What can you tell me about the dragon? Did it charge you? Breathe fire?"

"No. It...wanted the cow. Didn't even act as though it saw us. We ran away, but it didn't chase us. Still eating the cow. Like it was playing with its food."

"Describe it to me. Everything. Every detail!" he pressed. He pulled Tiffin to the small table in the room, pushing him into the chair and dipping a quill in ink. He yanked a sheet of blank parchment from the teetering pile in front of him, scratching the writing utensil across the page nearly as quickly as Tiffin spoke.

He described everything he could remember: the color, the horns and spikes, the shape of the wings, the estimated size, the smells, even its speed.

"And there was something at the bottom of its neck." He gestured to the hollow of his throat as he spoke.

"What kind of thing?"

He shrugged. "Something red. It was round, and it sort of...pulsed. Not bright red, but dark. Almost black."

Lifting his hand from the paper, the etherae squinted at Tiffin. "Red?" he repeated.

Tiffin's head bobbed in reply. "It wasn't very big, I think." He gestured with his hands to indicate the object's size. "But it was out of place. And I don't know how it was attached. I didn't see a rope or a chain or anything. Is that normal? It's the first stiguine I've seen in person."

The etherae stood so abruptly his chair fell over. He didn't bother righting it either, beginning to pace.

His father looked up hopefully. "What does that mean?"

His question went unanswered for nearly a minute. "I won't speculate yet. I must consult the others."

Aaron had crossed his arms over his chest, watching the whole exchange in disbelief. "How did this dragon that my sister has never seen poison her?"

"Ash." The word was so short. The etherae was pacing again, looking from the parchment to Tiffin and then into nothing.

"Ash," his father repeated. "I don't understand."

The etherae sighed and began to explain, his tone slow and even. "Anything burned up creates ash which gets swept up in the air and carried. We believe that it has reached the castle food supply now. We have taken extra precautions, washing everything that comes into the kitchens before it is prepared. All it takes is to ingest it. But it could have landed on her food or drink floating through a window while being delivered. Your sister must have ingested some."

"That *you* served her!" Aaron accused, bridging the distance between them in a few steps. "If you knew about the ash, why didn't you protect her?"

The etherae didn't budge, looking bored with the whole exchange. "I will ask you to back up," he ordered.

"You let my sister get infected!" Aaron accused, taking another step forward.

"Back up." This time, he lifted two fingers, folding his thumb over his fourth finger.

Tiffin held his breath as Aaron looked at the etherae and then to the guards clanking toward them. He exhaled as Aaron backed up one step.

The etherae blinked slowly and lowered his hand. "We are taking every precaution."

"What do we do now?" Aaron questioned. "I have to do something. I have to fix this."

"We are easing her pain. She is in the best possible circumstance for such an episode." He sighed. "There is a cure, but only a grand master has the ability to fashion it. And there is but one close enough to do it in time."

"So, let's get that person!" Aaron exclaimed, hands in the air. "My son is possibly the best and fastest rider in the village. We'll get him. Where can we go?"

The etherae sighed again. "We don't know. He's missing."

"Missing?" Tiffin and his father yelped.

Aaron lifted his hands to cover his face with a growl. "What are you doing around here? People falling sick? Missing? Who's in charge?" He threw his arms wide in consternation.

Tiffin grabbed his father's arm. "Dad, don't."

The old man watched the tantrum and folded his hands in front of himself.

"Because you are in pain, I will give you this one opportunity to control yourself before I allow this guard to haul you away for your insolence."

The etherae turned back to the table and picked up his chair. He righted it and took a seat, leaning on his elbows to stare at Tiffin. "You are the only person I've ever known who saw a stiguine attack up close and lived."

Tiffin remained silent, unsure what was expected of him. He was still reeling from the news about his aunt. There was a cure supposedly, but no one to make it. It sounded like an excuse to prevent him from having hope. How dare he be told about the cure if there was no way to make it?

"Are you saying that you can't save her?" he uttered.

"No." The etherae's answer had been swift. He sat up and

straightened his sleeves. "There is hope. Even if the grand master was accounted for, the cure requires an ingredient we have not successfully retrieved."

"I'll get it," Tiffin volunteered. He didn't care what it was. He would go to the ends of the earth for it if necessary.

"No," his father corrected. "I will. I cannot lose you both. You would be better here at her side."

"Dad, you told him I was the best horseman in the village. Let me do this," Tiffin pleaded.

"Your horsemanship is irrelevant," the etherae interjected. "It's a matter of finding the dragon. The stiguine that you saw with the cow. Do you have any experience tracking it?"

He shrugged sadly. "I've never tried." Of all the times for his dragon knowledge to fail him, he wanted to cry if it was what stood between him and saving his aunt.

"We need a stiguine dragon scale to make the potion that will cure her."

"Easy! I'll find its lair and sneak out some that it shed," Tiffin announced.

The etherae shook his head. "No. They have to be fresh. We believe the best plan is to find the dragon's lair and extract one while it is sleeping."

"That's suicide," his father exclaimed. "The second he pulls a scale off this giant creature, it will either burn him alive or eat him. Or both. That's a terrible plan. You can't send my son to die. Let me go with him."

The etherae did not have the courtesy to look bothered. "You will do nothing but slow him down. You are too large and too old."

Tiffin balked, looking from the old man to his much younger and healthier father. His father could do anything!

If he had realized his faux pas, the etherae gave no indication as he continued. "You are the smithy, yes?"

Aaron crossed his arms over his barrel chest, straightening his stance, showing off every inch of his six-foot-two frame.

"That's right."

"The best thing you can do is get this boy your best sword. Armor too, if you have it. How quickly can you work?"

Aaron's stance remained steadfast. "How fast do I need to?"

The etherae met his gaze without wavering. "He should leave today."

"And where is he supposed to even start?" Aaron quipped.

The etherae raised a finger and rushed back to the table, rifling through the disorganized pile. He flung one hand into the air, waving a parchment, and splayed a crude map on top of the pile.

"We have been collecting sightings of the beast since the fires started. We think it's making a loop. These other villages have sent word of similar terror." He circled the route on the map. "Where did you see him, boy?"

Tiffin scowled, indicating the spot. "It's the last pasture within a day's walk for cattle to graze."

"We think it must be nesting in this region." The old man pointed to the map again, indicating a mountainous area. "It's big enough to rest and still be close enough to terrorize the surrounding cities. We can think of no other suitable location for a beast this size."

"That's at least a two-day ride, maybe three," his father protested.

Under the circumstances, Tiffin estimated he could make it in less time. He was more concerned about how he was going to get hold of a dragon scale. "You're sure I have to pull it out? How am I supposed to do that?"

"Our best idea has been to sneak in while it sleeps and pluck out a scale like a hair from your head."

It sounded so easy. Find the dragon, catch it asleep, pull a scale, and run like the wind. But most things that sounded too good to be true often were. His brain twisted itself around the problem. Tracking something on the ground was one thing, but tracking something that could travel miles by air and leave no trace was another thing entirely. He stared at the map, translating the cartography to locations he was familiar with to narrow down the vicinity further.

Tiffin looked at his father and crossed his arms over his chest, adopting his father's daunting stance. "I'll do it."

Aaron stared back, lips tight and jaw clenching. He turned his gaze to the empowered man across from them. "And what are you doing about your missing etherae?"

"There is a squad searching for him. If anyone can find him, it will be them. We can prepare the other ingredients and have everything ready, but the cure itself takes half a day to complete. The sooner your aunt has the antidote, the better her chances will be."

His father paced the room. "I don't like this."

"It's Aunt Helen, Dad. What choice do we have? And how many others will be saved if I succeed?"

"I know." Aaron ran a hand over his head, pushing his unruly mass of hair back and behind his ears. "I'm going to get you some weapons and armor." He said nothing else, rushing out of the room.

Tiffin watched him go, suddenly unsure of what he should do next.

"Go to your aunt. Stay at her side. Your father will provide you with weapons. I will gather supplies for you here. When we finish, you will leave. Are you bonded to your steed?"

Tiffin nodded.

The etherae's expression changed from stern to sincere. He placed one hand on Tiffin's shoulder. "Go. Be with her. You have eight days to collect the scales. Every moment counts."

Chapter 4

Tiffin followed the guard back to his aunt's room. She was asleep again, and he sat next to her with one hand laid over hers.

In his whole life, he had never seen her this way. She was always vibrant. She sang when she thought no one was listening. She could turn simple stones into imaginary soldiers and leaves into forts. She could take the same flour he had tried to manipulate and turn it into bread and cakes and an assortment of other treats that he couldn't begin to name. He couldn't picture his life, or his father's, without her in it.

He stared at her long face. Her nose was narrow and straight, eyes set evenly on either side. Her lids were smooth, the lashes long over her blue-tinged cheeks. He watched her thin lips part as she exhaled a near-silent whimper.

Tiffin was unaware that he wasn't alone until the other side of the bed sagged. The princess reached for Helen's other hand, and Tiffin averted his eyes. He rarely interacted directly with her. They both pretended that he wasn't there during her lessons. Pretended that the snacks and lunches delivered to her quarters weren't disappearing when no one was looking.

When she spoke, her voice was like a morning bird filling the air with sweetness. "Do you know that your aunt taught me to knit? She's very good at it. She makes the most lovely shawls."

Tiffin shook his head.

"She means more to me than my own mother," the princess confessed. She took a lock of Helen's hair and curled it around her own finger then combed it out. "I always wondered why she hasn't married and left me."

"When Aunt Helen loves you, she loves all of you forever," Tiffin clarified. "Even if she did marry, she wouldn't leave you."

They were silent for a spell, and when the princess spoke, her voice was nearly a whisper.

"I don't want her to die."

"Me either. I'll find the dragon scale they need to make the cure."

"Do you really think you can?" she asked, looking full on him.

"I have to, don't I?" he mumbled, looking back at his aunt.

The princess leaned toward him slightly, and in the next moment, she was pressing something into his hand. It was roughly the length of his palm, but it wasn't until he glanced down that he understood what she had passed him.

"Where were you hiding this?" he burst out, concealing the small knife quickly by slipping it up his sleeve. He glanced around to see who had seen the transaction, but the guards were seemingly unaware. Helen didn't even flinch.

"In my boot," she giggled quietly. Her dimple punctuated her words. "Your aunt gave it to me so I would never be unguarded. And if you are to succeed, you will need all the assistance you can get."

He frowned, moving his hand a few inches toward her. "Then you truly will be unguarded."

She shook her head, ignoring his gesture. "It is all of myself I can send with you." She caught his eyes plaintively. "You can't fail."

He sucked in a breath at the way her eyes seemed to bore into him. "I won't."

Princess Narette did not linger, leaving Tiffin alone with his aunt. Different etherae came and went, treating his aunt with tender care and mopping her face.

When his father nudged him awake that evening, he was surprised he had been asleep. His head was on the bed against her hand, and as he woke, she pulled away. He kissed her forehead and followed his father into the hallway.

"She was so healthy yesterday," he mused.

He could see the streaks where tears had made clean paths in the dirt stretching from his father's eyes into his beard, and he didn't press the issue further.

"I've been making this for your birthday this year, but I didn't want you to know." He pulled a dark bag from over his shoulder and extracted first a chain mail shirt then a thin, long sword unlike any he had seen before. "Your aunt gave me the idea for this when she was mending. Poked a needle halfway into her finger before she even noticed she'd done it. So, I made a sword like it." He held the item out.

Tiffin took it in awe. The blade was narrow, almost cylindrical, but it was shaped like a star, each of the edges sharp and wicked looking. He could imagine shoving it through an opponent and all the havoc twisting it would wreak. He glanced at his father's heavy brow and wondered what he thought this journey was going to be.

"Quick, see if it fits. I can adjust some of the rings if I have to, but I need to know now, son."

Tiffin passed the blade back and accepted the chain mail. It was remarkably heavy for being composed of tiny rings. He draped it over his neck, then slipped his arms into the long sleeves. The rings reached his knuckles and swung below his hips. He looked to his father for approval.

The older man didn't break a smile, but he plucked at the shoulders and under the arms.

"Please be fast and quiet, and whatever you do, don't die. Even if it means that you don't get the dragon scale. Promise me that you won't die."

Tiffin glanced back at the door between them and his aunt. "No one can promise that, Dad. I can promise that I will be fast and smart, and I promise to pay attention and take a bath at every chance."

His father let out a single laugh, then clamped his arms around his son in a hug. "I love you, Tiffin, down to every last hair on your head."

Tiffin could barely breathe, but he squeezed back hard.

They were interrupted by the etherae clattering up to them, papers clutched in hand.

"Ah! Good work. I see you've received your tools from your father." He thrust the papers into Tiffin's hands.

The etherae grabbed him by the shoulders, leading him toward a well-concealed stairwell and ushering him down the steps. His next words were hurried, and Tiffin almost didn't understand him.

"I've had supplies loaded to your horse. These papers show ingredients you should gather along the way if you can. We have most in great supply, but fresh is always best. If you can get more than one scale, boy, do," he instructed.

"Look—I've told him not to die, even if it means Helen doesn't make it," Aaron admitted.

The etherae stopped, all three stumbling in his haste. "No. He must succeed. And for more than Helen. If this dragon continues—we will all die."

Aaron grumbled and caught Tiffin's eye with a single shake of his head.

They started moving again and didn't stop until they'd reached Gertrude, saddlebags full and even a bedroll.

The etherae cringed as he looked down at Tiffin. "I'm sorry. I've not even asked your name."

"Tiffin," he replied softly.

"I am Bastian," the etherae introduced. "Please forgive my haste tonight that has superseded my manners. Under other circumstances, I would have addressed you differently."

"As in, not at all," his father interrupted.

The two older men exchanged sour looks before the etherae turned back to Tiffin. "Have you any ethereal skills or training?"

Tiffin shook his head. "No, sir, but I've always wanted to."

"If you can survive this, young one, I will make the arrangements and oversee your studies myself."

He had always wanted a mentor, always wanted to be called out for something he was good at. But now, when it was happening, he wasn't sure he deserved it. He glanced at his father, who was packing away his sword near the bedroll.

Tiffin hugged his father one more time before mounting his horse and felt his father grip his calf once he was settled. He looked down on Aaron, studying the tiny bare spot forming on the back of his head.

The etherae was the only one who spoke. "You know which way you're headed?"

"I have a plan," he assured.

The etherae offered him a slight bow. "Be safe, child. And know that your kingdom is at your mercy," he offered.

Tiffin spurred his mount forward, taking advantage of the lights of the city to clear the castle gates. The light behind him made eerie shadows of the trees as he followed the road, but they soon faded, leaving him in moonlight.

He focused his gaze on the mountains ahead. Everything he needed was only as far away as their white-peaked caps. They were dark in the distance, foreboding as they scraped the sky. If the dragon was holed up there, he wondered what other manner of thing was waiting for him ahead. He plodded along as the stars guided him toward their dark base.

Part of him was grateful to be alone. It had been startlingly difficult to sit next to his sick aunt and listen to her labored breathing and regular whimpers of pain. He had split his time thinking about her illness, the map, and his knowledge of the surrounding forests. He hadn't planned on napping, but as he and Gertrude made haste, he was grateful for the extra energy.

They traveled quickly as far as the road would allow before

veering off. His horse, it seemed, had not had the luxury of the same nap he had, and she was slowing down.

The trees of the forest closed in around him, the starlight vanishing beneath the canopy. He patted her mane gently.

"Alright, Gertrude. Let's go to bed. I've got this new bedroll and everything."

Tiffin's legs were stiff as he dismounted and pulled the packs from his horse. The bags were heavy, and he grunted as he controlled their fall. They were loaded with salted meat, bread, cheese, potato cakes, fresh vegetables, and two flasks. He found a small pot as well. It reminded him of all the times he'd watched his aunt prepare stew. He didn't expect what he put in the pot would taste anything like hers, but at least it was something. The staff had brought him a meager bowl of soup which had been intended for his aunt. However, when she couldn't eat, he devoured its contents, but it hadn't improved the gnawing feeling.

With Gertrude tied loosely nearby, grazing happily and quietly, Tiffin spared no time organizing his campsite while chewing on a mouthful of cheese to abate his hunger. He built a fire and set about making a small stew.

The forest creaked around him as the wind picked up speed. Tiny creatures rustled in the grass. The aroma of the beef plumping up and the vegetables softening as the water boiled made him drool. He wanted very much to pull it from the fire and eat it right away. Instead, he laid out his pallet and sorted through the goods in his keep.

In the fire's light, he could barely make out the drawings Bastian had pressed into his hands as he departed. The sketches were intricate, detailing the color and quantity of each item. There were even special collection bags inside the packs for individual ingredients. How he was supposed to make haste and gather plants, he wasn't certain.

A twig snapped behind him, and he fought every instinct to whirl around. Tiffin held his breath, then stood slowly and stirred the pot. As he did, he scanned the area for an indication of what had made the noise. He casually squatted near the fire, searching the scrub behind where he had been sitting.

It took a moment, but when he saw it, he locked in. A pair of yellow eyes stared back, and Tiffin waited for the wolf attached to them to growl territorially. However, there was only the sound of panting.

Shuffling, Tiffin approached, his eyes adjusting to the dark and distinguishing the multi-colored fur. The wolf's mouth hung open, tongue lolling to one side as it regarded him.

He looked around, a little less wary now that he had found the culprit. He could see no other critters or people. He sighed, gazing back down at the creature.

"I suppose you're hungry and smelled my dinner," he told his visitor.

Tiffin could have sworn the wolf smiled at him as it stared up at him.

"Come on, then. I've got some extras," he offered, going back to his original spot. He listened to the crackling of the foliage as the wolf followed.

Tiffin stared in disbelief. He'd never heard of a friendly feral wolf. In fact, he had been told there was no such thing. But here it was, following along beside him as calm as Gertrude. The wolf stopped near the bedroll as Tiffin approached the fire to check on his dinner. The liquid had reduced by at least a third and swirled thickly around the vegetables. With a sturdy stick, he lifted the pot from the fire.

He pulled a chunk of bread from the satchel, tore off a piece, and held it out to his new friend.

The wolf met his eyes, drawing minutely closer to sniff the offering. He sneezed on it, drew back, and sat on his haunches.

Tiffin turned his nose up at the resulting gelatinous crust, glad he'd offered a small piece, and tossed it to the ground. He supposed some other animal might be more grateful for the find in the morning. If he was the wolf, he would want the meat. Tiffin wanted the meat very badly himself.

He allowed his dinner to cool then turned out a portion of it on the ground near the bread.

The wolf stared at it dumbly, and Tiffin shrugged. "Suit yourself. It's what I've got. If you try it, you might like it."

As the words left his lips, he heard his aunt's voice coaxing him into trying new foods as he got older. He pictured the way she'd turn away from him, brows arched and looking down her nose at whatever was at hand before glancing at him. Her whole face would burst into a smile if he tried it, even if he didn't like it. "Good on you for trying," she'd encourage.

He sighed, dipping his bread into the soup and sampling it timidly. It wasn't bad. Out of the corner of his eye, he saw the wolf lick at the wet food, then lap it up hungrily until nothing was left but a muddy spot. Even the bread was gone. The wolf sat back and stared at him, licking its chops.

Tiffin laughed, tension oozing from his body. Overwhelmed by his tasks and worn by the long ride to his current location, he wanted to pass out.

He was indeed fortunate to have found such a companion. When he had finished a bit more than half of his dinner, he dumped the rest out for his friend. Maybe, if the wolf stayed nearby with a full belly, he would be protected.

His father would never believe him if he told him he'd spent the night with a wolf at his side. He could hardly believe it himself. He tossed more fuel on his fire, satisfied that it would last at least till he fell asleep, then rolled himself up in his bedroll the best he could and drifted into unconsciousness.

He dreamed of the dragon attack that he and Gimble had survived. He remembered the great rushing of wind as its wings flapped; the way its body glimmered as each scale moved independently of the others. They had both a unity and a distinction that set each one apart. Its neck was exceedingly long, curling into an S shape and twisting in mesmerizing, gyrating patterns. He allowed his eyes to trail from the tip of one wing all the way to the tip of the other. Great bones framed each. Near its body, they were as thick as his father's thigh, and at the ends, as thin as his own fingers.

The skin between them was thicker at the base as well, nearly translucent at the point where it reached the smaller bones. The whole expanse flexed against the air, first concave, then convex. The creature had not flapped them often—only three or four beats before it would soar like a bird, catching currents invisible to the eye. Tiffin imagined it like a fish moving through water. Every fiber of the dragon's body was attuned to its environment, shifting instinctively to meet each change. The effect was nothing short of graceful.

But this time, when the creature dove down to take Trudy, she wasn't there. Instead, Tiffin was staring deep into the great maw, which housed three rows of razor-sharp teeth the size of boulders. The teeth ranged widely in size, largest in the front, and smallest in the back. A great, pointed, black tongue wriggled inside, and Tiffin's belly tightened hungrily. His soul cried out to be set free, and he shivered with the need for revenge. Overarching all of this was despair, deep inside, more damaging than the teeth that threatened to swallow him whole.

Just before the giant jaw could snap around him, Tiffin woke in a sweat, gasping for air and letting out a yelp.

The wolf on the other side of the remaining embers of his campfire startled awake, jumping instantly to his feet and searching around for the threat that had scared Tiffin to consciousness. As if sensing something, his new companion darted back into the forest.

Tiffin caught his breath, coughing a little as the wind directed the fire's smoke in his direction. It was still dark, but he could see the sun's first light illuminating the road.

With no time to waste, he broke down camp, wrestled the full saddlebags onto his horse, and set out again toward the mountains. His ride was slower this time, as he blazed his own trail through the tight network of trees. Gertrude didn't seem to mind, and they passed the morning quietly. By the time the sun was high in the sky, he was sweating horribly, shrugging under the weight of the chain mail.

The sound of water in the distance perked his ears, and he swore Gertrude picked up the pace as he directed her to the sound. As expected, he found a fresh stream, and Gertrude nearly threw him in as she rushed toward it. She stopped at its banks, drinking deeply.

Once free of her back, Tiffin divested himself of the chain mail and jumped in, feeling the cold water seep through his hair to his scalp, shocking his senses as the heat abruptly fled his body. He sucked in water by the handful until he thought his belly would burst. If he had not been on a mission, he thought his father might like this place. Perhaps his aunt, too. He imagined them having a picnic on its shore and frowned. He had a mission. Only boys would stop to play in the water when so much was at stake.

Tiffin waded to the shore, pulling maps and food from his pack to eat while he studied. It took some turning, but Tiffin found the path on the parchment, tracing it with his finger. There were few landmarks to judge, but he was much closer to the mountains now. He needed to find a path either through or around them. He was certain Gertrude would not be able to climb over, and he wasn't sure he could either. He hadn't had much experience scaling mountains, and the little he had was all arms and legs flailing and never finding purchase. Surely, there would be some natural path up and over. If the trees could find a way to get there, he could too. His aunt was counting on him, and he'd promised Princess Narette.

Gertrude was grazing again, but her breathing had eased to her normal speed, and Tiffin hoped it had been enough time for her to rest. They had never ridden so much in a day, and without her, he was reduced to walking. She was critical to the journey.

He mounted again, following the river's edge until he found a safe crossing. The mountain loomed closer with every step, and he was grateful to find a rather large clearing. Gertrude wouldn't be held back, and she raced across it, shaking her head as she did.

Chapter 5

By the time the stars were dotting the sky again, the pair had reached the base of the mountain. Tiffin found shelter for the night in a cave large enough for Gertrude to clomp into, and the sound of her shoes against the stone echoed across the countryside. Tiffin managed a small fire at the mouth of his temporary home before setting up his bedroll and starting a pot of stew.

He watched the water boiling with the meat and vegetables as he had the night before and studied the papers from the etherae again, wondering how they had come across this information. He supposed everything that happened had happened before at some point in history. He had heard about the plague before his birth, but he had never experienced anything like it.

Shadows moved in the corner of his eye, and he glanced over to see the wolf from the night before slinking into the stone cavern.

"Oh, so you come for dinner?" Tiffin laughed.

The wolf padded toward him, stopping about a foot away, slightly out of his reach. He sat down on his haunches and stared, looking between the fire and Tiffin, waiting.

After their dinner, Tiffin settled into his bedroll, thinking it was far less comfortable on the stone floor. However, the stone had warmed with proximity to the fire, and his aching muscles loosened. When he woke, it wasn't from the dream, but from the sound of clanking.

His eyes popped open, darting around.

The wolf was already on all fours, lowered to the ground. A nearly inaudible growl rumbled in its throat. From where he lay, motionless in his bed, Tiffin could only see the animal's haunches shifting from one side to the other as it gauged its prey. It was protecting him.

Slowly, creating as little sound as possible, Tiffin crawled free of the sack, reaching for the sword from his father. He nearly had it unsheathed when Wolf leaped forward, snapping and growling more warnings.

Tiffin suddenly saw three men approaching, armor covering their tender bits. They were soldiers.

When Wolf leaped, the man on the receiving end shrieked, jumping backwards and nearly falling down.

Another pulled the man free before Wolf could grab him. The third pulled a sword from his hip, brandishing it at the wolf menacingly.

"Wait! Stop!" Tiffin cried, jumping to his feet. He charged the two nearest the animal, pointing his own sword. "Leave it alone. It's defending me! Who are you, sneaking up on us in the middle of the night?"

All three held up their hands defensively. "We mean you no harm. We were cold and saw your fire," they confessed.

The man speaking was unlike anyone Tiffin had ever seen before. His skin was the color of mahogany, and his hair was cropped close, nearly shaved on the sides. His eyes were wide, white orbs in the night air. The soldier knelt, very still, as the wolf circled him, growling.

Tiffin frowned. "I don't have anything to steal," he blurted. "And this wolf is my friend. You won't harm him."

One of the other men moved closer, slowly, hands still raised. This man was shorter, stouter, and his long, dark hair was tied back in a messy ponytail. Tiffin did not want to tangle with this man.

"You have a horse, fire, food...and a fairly fierce defense system."

Tiffin scowled. "I have a sword, and should you push me, I'm not afraid to press you." He thought of the princess's blade concealed in his boot.

The third man had the audacity to laugh. His olive toned skin was topped with short coal black hair and his face was punctuated with a wide mouth. All his teeth showed.

"You would press us, little one? Truly?"

At this, Tiffin brandished his sword, grateful to be wearing the chain shirt. His father's foresight gave his spine some fortitude as he bounced lightly from his right foot to his left and back to limber up his muscles.

At this, all three laughed, flinching only when the wolf planted itself in front of Tiffin, baring all his teeth.

"We are knights, young squire," the first man explained. "We are on a quest, and we lost our supplies."

"Because someone is bad at cards," the knight with the ponytail clarified, giving a sidelong glance at the olive-skinned man.

"I was great," the man countered. "I can't help it that it was all a distraction to sneak away with our stuff. You didn't see it happening either, so don't blame me!"

Tiffin watched them bickering, and the wolf eased back, slowly settling at his feet. Away from the fire now, the night's chill wheedled its way to his bones, and he sympathized with these men clad in metal. He couldn't turn them away. He lowered his sword.

"I only have one horse, and she's mine," Tiffin demanded. "But I can share my fire for the night."

"That is all we need," said the dark-skinned man. "Thank you." He gestured to his companions. "Elias is a cunning hunter; Kaiden's gathering skills are second to none. We can find our own food."

"And Pierce's eating knows no bounds," Kaiden finished.

Tiffin rolled his eyes. These were grown men! At least his father's age, he suspected. How had they managed to lose all their wares on a quest? He turned, resuming his place in his bedroll and settling down. He tucked his sword next to him, hoping he didn't roll into it. But with a cave full of strangers, he was willing to risk it. Hopefully, he wasn't endangering his own quest by giving these supposed knights succor.

He watched through one eye as they dismantled themselves, surprisingly quiet for all the metal. They set each piece down gently, barely making a noise before squeezing close to the fire.

Tiffin studied their armor, noting the intricate adornment. It looked like the armor from the castle, though he had never seen these men before. And their status as knights on its own did not make them honorable.

Exhaustion finally won him over, and despite the potential threats, Tiffin drifted back into sleep. He dreamed again of the dragon, this time his attention focused on the red stone at the base of its neck. He swore he saw the faint outline of a face on its surface before he was eaten and woke up in a cold sweat.

Wolf lifted his head, gave him a gimlet gaze, then rested it back on his enormous, furry paws.

Catching his breath, Tiffin stared out across the forest, trying to forget the wet hot breath blowing his hair from his forehead. What did it all mean?

He wanted a bite of bread and cheese, but he feared that if he pulled it out in front of his guests, they'd be hungry too. While he usually was the first to share, Tiffin wasn't sure how long his quest would go on. His aunt was counting on him to get a dragon scale and save her life. He *needed* all his food.

He began packing up his bedroll. The sooner he got on the road, the sooner he could eat something. Gertrude was nearby, flicking her tail occasionally to ward off pesky flies. She seemed anxious to set out on their own again.

Once she was loaded, Tiffin led Gertrude from their

hideout quietly. She even stepped lightly, her shoes making the barest clack against the floor, which was still warm from the remains of the fire. He glanced at the knights, snoring and peaceful, and wondered how long they had been searching for their quarry. It was unusual to see men sleeping so long and late, especially directly on a stone floor as they had been.

His heart strings tugged at their plight. They had eaten nothing the night before, only passed out in the warmth. He reached into his bag, pulled out a wrapped loaf of bread and set it where his bedroll had been. They would certainly be hungry, and one loaf for all three of them was a paltry offering. But it would be rude to leave them with nothing given their state of affairs.

He waited till they had put some distance between himself and the knights before he hopped on Gertrude's back and began to pick his way up the steep mountain's side. Traveling was slow, and he knew soon he would need to lead Gertrude up instead of ride. His hips ached, and his bones ground against one another with the constant jarring of the horse's footsteps beneath him.

Today, he was aware of the wolf keeping pace with them, mostly out of sight, but he was growing used to the creature's companionship. He sensed it easily, grateful for the way it covered their scent.

The sun was high in the sky, and Tiffin groaned when he drained the last few drops of water from his flask. He would have to find a refill, and he consulted the map as Gertrude trotted along hoping to see signs of water anywhere on the crudely drawn sketch.

The Fates must have been on his side as he spied a stream in the near distance and set on the path to meet it.

His stomach rumbled as he refilled the flask. Gertrude drank deeply beside him on the left, the wolf on his right. He splashed the water over his face and head, shivering as cool rivulets ran down his neck and into the back of his shirt. He considered jumping in as he had done the day before, but he would have to strip off the chain mail, and he didn't think it prudent to do so with strangers so near.

Wolf growled low in the back of his throat, freezing with his head near the stream. His companion's ear twitched in opposite directions. He lifted his head slowly, the rumble growing louder.

Tiffin spied his guests from the previous night and faced them. He resisted crossing his arms over his chest to convey his dislike of being followed. Instead, with his aunt's repeated corrections about his stance, he placed his hands on his hips as he stared them down.

"It's the young squire," Kaiden called out merrily.

"I'm no one's squire," Tiffin snapped. "If I didn't know better, I'd think you were following me." How had they caught up to him so fast without horses?

His fingertips rested on the sword at his hip. The simple touch of flesh to metal bolstered his confidence.

Pierce laughed at the display, and Tiffin was strongly starting to think he did not like the laugh.

"Still your hand, young sir. We mean you no harm. We are glad to see you again to thank you for your generous offer. The bread has given us a good start today."

He could hardly continue snarling at someone thanking him. "It was the least I could do," he mumbled.

"What is your quest exactly?" Elias asked. "I'm beginning to wonder if these run-ins are fated and not coincidence."

Tiffin eyed them warily. So far, they had acted as knights in their position should, outside of losing their gear, and he couldn't see the harm in sharing his burden.

"I am searching for the dragon plaguing our lands to get

a scale fresh from its body."

Three pairs of eyes opened wide, and at least one jaw dropped.

"How old are you?" Kaiden questioned.

Tiffin stood a little taller, gripping his sword's hilt. "Fourteen," he replied. "Very nearly a man. Not a young squire at all."

Pierce's face contorted into a smirk as his eyes reduced to something nearer their normal size, and he rested both hands on the butt-end of his broad sword.

"Forgive our misunderstanding. I see that you are an accomplished man in your own right. Tell us more about this dragon if you don't mind," Pierce requested.

Tiffin considered for a long moment. They had shown up unexpectedly in the dark last night, and his hackles were raised. However, even in their surprise appearance, they had been nothing but honorable.

Upon their most recent arrival, they had taken every precaution with their words and actions to put his mind at ease. He studied each of them in turn, near motionless awaiting his reply. And with a sick turning in the pit of his stomach, he understood that if the three of them wanted to harm him, there was very likely nothing he could do about it, sword or not. It served his purpose better to enlist their aid rather than proceed stubbornly on his own.

He shared the details he knew about the dragon, the poison, and finally, the real reason he wanted to find a cure: his fatally infected aunt.

"She has the sickness," he explained. "Master Bastian says that if I can retrieve a scale from the dragon, there is an etherae who can make the cure. I left her two nights ago.

She's in so much pain, but she didn't want me to know."

"Aunts are stoic like that, trying to keep you from worrying," Pierce sympathized. "I take it you're close."

Tiffin nearly choked on the air. "She's raised me practically since I was born. Mom...I never knew her. It's been Aunt Helen and Dad and me all this time."

The knights bowed their heads, Elias kissing a medallion around his neck and lifting it skyward.

"I'd do anything for her," Tiffin added.

Kaiden's eyebrows drew together, and his arms crossed loosely over himself. He glanced at his fellow knights. "The Fates have placed us in one another's paths. I am sure of it."

Elias and Pierce nodded agreement. "It appears our quests align," Pierce confirmed. "You seek the dragon scales for the potion. We seek the etherae who can wield them. We did not realize there was a dragon involved in the cure. And knowing that it also requires our good friend makes his disappearance smell quite different than the random kidnapping we were led to believe."

The knights shared concerned expressions.

Tiffin sensed the same connection Pierce indicated, but how the pieces of the puzzle fit together, he was uncertain.

"The dragon wouldn't be poisoning villages for no reason," Tiffin rationalized. "Do you think someone's controlling it? Who would do that? Who *could* do that?"

"Who indeed?" Pierce concurred. He pursed his lips, glancing from Tiffin to the knights. "I believe you need our help and we need yours."

If the knights could get him closer to saving his aunt, he was all in. But he worried that combining their quests would only slow him down. "Master Bastian said time was limited.

I must make getting this scale my priority."

"But your scale without the etherae to use it is worthless. The grand master etherae you need is our good friend Darius," Pierce pointed out. "Finding him is *our* priority."

Elias continued. "If Darius and the dragon are connected to the same scheme, and it sounds like they are, I expect one will be close to the other."

It was difficult to deny the logic. "And your path has led to me?"

Elias bowed his head in the affirmative. "I assume you believe you aren't just wondering aimlessly. You know where this dragon is?"

Pulling the maps from his saddle bags, Tiffin showed them the path Bastian had indicated before he had fled the castle two days prior. "Master Bastian says it will take less than a fortnight before the sickness will overcome her, and her body will give up the fight," he added. "He gave me eight days to return with the scale so they have time to make the potion. Whatever I do, I can't waste any time. I have five days left."

Elias patted his shoulder. "I understand, but I see how you're walking, and you need some time out of the saddle. Let's eat, and then we will find this dragon."

Tiffin sighed. If he got too sore to move, he'd never reach the dragon, or if he did, he wouldn't be able to make it back, and his aunt needed him. For all she had done for him, he owed her.

"I...I don't have a lot of food left," he stammered. "The castle only gave me enough for *my* quest."

Elias reached behind his hip, pulling something from his belt, and Tiffin was shocked to see a trio of rabbits.

Tiffin cringed, not used to seeing the creatures he so enjoyed eating before they had been cooked.

The olive-skinned man smirked. "City boy," he teased. "Breakfast was on you. Lunch is on us."

Feeling abruptly indebted to these men appearing out of nowhere and offering to cook for him, Tiffin scrambled to match their generosity. "I've got some vegetables left. Carrots, I think," he offered.

Kaiden's face brightened. "I love carrots," he enthused. He pulled a pouch from his hip. "This will help. And I've got precisely the right herb for the saddle soreness. Fixes everything," he explained, following after Elias. "You still have your boot knife, right?"

"Of course," Elias grumbled.

Tiffin couldn't hear the rest as they disappeared downstream, and Tiffin looked away as Elias strung the rabbits up by their feet and began cleaning them with a small knife he pulled from his boot.

The sight called Tiffin to the vague awareness of the hard blade from the princess near his ankle and fought the urge to reach for it. The princess would never forgive him if he failed. In fact, she could in her capricious nature, have him punished for his failure, and he was incredibly fond of the current location of his head.

He turned to his saddle bags, rifling through till he found his remaining vegetables and pulled them free. They were beginning to soften in the saddle bags, and he thought he would rather share them than let them go to waste. He was keenly aware of Pierce watching him and felt slightly unnerved for no obvious reason as he set the food near where the other man was building a fire.

"For someone on his first quest, you are impressively supplied," Pierce noted as he stacked twigs inside a loose ring of stones.

Tiffin shrugged. "I can't take credit. Master Bastian had the saddlebags prepared for the journey."

"Your aunt must be someone special," Pierce pointed out as he began striking a pair of rocks together. Large sparks rained over the kindling, and in no time, there was fire. "Bastian rarely intervenes on anyone's behalf."

"She's the princess's companion," Tiffin explained, feeling pride tug up one corner of his mouth.

"Wow. She *is* important." Pierce tossed a larger piece into the fire and pressed it into place. "Princess Narette is quite a handful, and they say her companion is the greatest peacekeeper to live."

Tiffin shrugged. "She's important to me and my dad."

"But she's important to the kingdom, too." Pierce remained still next to the fire as he started feeding larger logs into the flames, eyeing the wolf poised at the edge of the stream.

The creature was crouched and quietly watching his every move. "And did you bring him from home?" The knight gestured toward the furry animal.

"No, he invited himself along the first night when I was cooking. I guess he liked the smell of my stew." Tiffin chuckled.

"I've never seen a wild wolf this close before. You must have very high-level marks in your animal training," Pierce noted.

"I don't have any marks. I'm too busy herding goats and shoeing horses. My father is the smithy. But, if I am successful, and my aunt lives, Bastian said he would mentor me himself."

Pierce waved a hand and blew raspberries. "The man we're looking for, Darius, is a *true* etherae. He's leagues above Bastian. He might be royal, but he's barely a master. As etherae go...Darius is past the one hundredth level. They stopped measuring him years ago. Born with most of it, but he's the fastest learner I've ever encountered," Pierce bragged. "He would be a far better mentor."

Tiffin's eyes went wide. He had never met a person above the one hundredth level before. He had begun to think they didn't really exist. He had no way of knowing if what Pierce said was true.

"If he's so smart, why can't he work out how to escape wherever he is?" Tiffin probed. "Are you sure he's been taken? Maybe he's hiding out somewhere till the dragon threat is over."

The knight scowled. "The only reason I will allow you to say that is because you don't know Darius. I assure you—he is taken. He has never run from danger before. Usually, he is the first to step in."

"I'm sorry," Tiffin said. "You're right. I don't know him."

Pierce threw the last log on the fire and sat back. His gaze was far away. "His quarters were completely torn apart. I worry that he was injured in the struggle. I am unsure how he was taken so quietly otherwise. People can be very smart and still rendered unconscious."

"Oh," Tiffin muttered. "I didn't think of that."

"Hyper intelligence is not the same as brute force," Pierce explained. "But out of all the grand master etherae known, I believe Darius to be the most powerful. I'm certain if we can find him, he can heal your aunt."

Tiffin sighed relief. "Well, I hope we find him."

"I believe his disappearance and your dragon are connected. He is probably near your quarry anyway. I feel we are safer together than apart. I am still in shock that you were sent alone."

"I'm a great rider, and I know a lot about dragons."

"But what if you had run into bandits or had an accident?" Pierce reasoned. "I know you're in a hurry, but it's foolish to send you with no protection."

Tiffin gestured to his sword and plucked at his chain mail shirt. "I have protection."

Pierce raised a hand to concede.

Stretching uncomfortably, Tiffin twisted at the waist in a futile attempt to ease the pain in his backside.

"Let me help you. Every knight has gone through this particular trial at the outset of his training. Do this." Pierce placed his hands on his hips for balance then did some slow lunges, keeping his back straight.

Tiffin thought he looked ridiculous, but he tried anyway, shocked when the muscles in pain were pulled, and it both hurt and provided relief. After several repetitions, Pierce showed him a few others. The last one involved lying on his back with his knees to his chest, and he groaned in pain and delight.

Kaiden and Elias smiled as they returned, Elias with an arm full of twigs and firewood. "I see you're showing him the tricks."

Pierce leaped to his feet, brushing off the forest from his back. He stoked the fire while Tiffin stretched till the worst of the pain eased. Since they would be stopped for longer than planned, Tiffin unloaded Gertrude and pulled out the papers to review again.

"What's that?" Kaiden asked as he spitted his catch and arranged it over the fire.

"Herbs and ingredients that Bastian asked me to pick if I found any. I haven't had much luck. I've been trying to go fast, and looking for flowers is not my priority."

Boldly, Kaiden took the papers from him. "There's a whole patch of this back that way," he offered. "Plants I'm good at."

"*Good*," Elias mocked. "What he means to say is he's a level sixty-three herbologist. His good is like most people's luckiest day."

Kaiden grinned shyly and shrugged. "I'm good at what I'm good at." He waved one of the pages at Tiffin. "I'll go grab some after we eat. It's a bit prickly to collect if you've never touched it before."

"Thank you," Tiffin replied in awe. The people in his village were nice enough, but none of them were kind like any of these men. Despite sneaking up on him in the night, Elias, Kaiden, and Pierce had done nothing but treat him like a brother.

Kaiden's skills allowed him to prepare their food so quickly, it felt like no time at all before he instructed them all to get started while he went picking the herbs that Tiffin needed for the antidote.

"I'm still surprised that the castle sent you out here alone," Pierce noted once more as he tucked into his food. "Can't quite get my head around it."

"Bastian said time was something we didn't have and that

my father would only slow me down. He stayed behind to look after my aunt, who is his sister."

Pierce frowned. "What about her husband? He could've stayed with her or come with you."

Tiffin's brow furrowed. "She doesn't have one," he replied.

He licked his fingers in thought, relishing the last bits and crumbs of cheese and bread. They hadn't been exaggerating Kaiden's skills. Somehow, he had taken the usually gamey rabbits, added something he found growing in the forest, and suddenly, the flavors were alive.

"I don't know where she'd meet anyone," Tiffin continued. "She spends all her time with the princess or me or Dad. But she's the nicest woman walking this earth. When she didn't come home, we got worried and went to the castle. And I got sent here."

Pierce patted his shoulder. "She's not gone yet," he comforted. He rinsed his hands in the stream and stood. "Let's get to it. We need to find a dragon."

Tiffin was already on his feet. He loaded his papers back into the saddle bags, adjusted everything, and climbed atop his horse the moment they had the fire tamped out and covered in dirt.

"This way," he instructed, setting off at an easy pace as Gertrude picked through the uneven terrain.

"How do you know that?" Elias asked, clanging behind him.

"I just do," he replied. "And Gertrude thinks so, too." He didn't wait for them to protest, simply urged his horse ahead. All his life, he'd made remarks like that to family and friends or customers. He knew what the chickens wanted. He knew what the goats needed. Knew where Gertrude liked to be scratched. Everyone looked at him as though he'd grown a third eye, and he had grown weary of their disbelief. If they simply paid attention, they would be privy to all the same details.

Even now, as they rode, he had some sense of where the stiguine was resting. The way the air moved around them, tinging everything with a hint of sulfur, suggested that something fiery was nearby. Plus, the dreams he'd witnessed for the last two nights had to mean something. He had to trust himself. Bastian would never have sent him on this quest if he didn't think it was possible.

The three knights kept pace on foot better than Tiffin thought they would. He focused on sensing the dragon and watching his footing. Gertrude assisted with the latter, requiring barely a nudge left or right to keep going.

Suddenly, Elias grabbed her reins, jerking her head to one side. She neighed in dissent, front legs rising off the ground. It was roughly six inches or so, but Tiffin struggled to remain on her back.

"What is it?" Pierce whispered, rushing to his side.

Kaiden lifted a finger to his lips as he met Tiffin's eyes.

"Something's not right," Elias warned. "Do you smell smoke?"

"It's probably the dragon," Tiffin whispered, leaning down toward them.

Elias shook his head. "Firewood." He crept forward, gesturing for them to stay where they were.

Tiffin had no problem with this concept, watching Elias slink away.

The knight's posture was low to the ground, a dagger

drawn from his boot in one hand, the other poised on the hilt of his broadsword. Despite his crouched position, he moved quickly, rounding the corner and using the brush to hide himself.

Everything was silent, and Tiffin looked at the others who were frozen, statue-like, eyes following their brother in arms. If they trusted him, he probably should too. He laid a hand on the side of Gertrude's neck to soothe her as she shifted beneath him, not understanding why they'd stopped.

Elias stood suddenly, his hands falling to his sides. He turned to the group. "Come on," he encouraged.

Tiffin, Kaiden, and Pierce edged forward as one, closing the distance quickly. It was then that Tiffin noticed the white smoke of a recently extinguished fire, the embers at the center of the makeshift pit still glowing red. Around the fire were four men, throats slit, blood slowly rolling into the remains of the coals and sizzling as it touched.

Clamping a hand over his mouth, Tiffin turned away. It was more gruesome seeing the aftermath of this fight than to have watched the stiguine bite a cow in half, and he'd had blood and guts raining down on him after that episode. But this was people, not animals, and part of his brain imagined that it could have been him and his father with Gimble and his father sitting around that same campfire and suddenly gone through a random act of violence.

"This was recent," Elias announced, and Tiffin noticed he had not put away the dagger.

Pierce gestured at the embers and looked around cautiously. "You'd think we'd have heard it. We weren't far away."

Elias crouched near one of the saddle bags and flipped

the leather flap aside, revealing a full bag. "This clearly wasn't a robbery. Too much left behind."

"Then why kill them at all?" Kaiden questioned.

The knights searched the remaining camp for some indication of who the men had been but turned up nothing.

Elias shook his head. "Whoever did it was quick and quiet. We should be on the lookout."

Tiffin glanced at the wolf that was still close by. If anyone had been scouting them, they hadn't alerted him, and Tiffin took some comfort in that. "All the more reason to keep going," he suggested.

"The kid's right," Kaiden agreed. "And I do not want to appear cold to these gruesome murders, but we should gather supplies while we can. They're not using them anymore, and we're supply poor."

The knights glanced at one another briefly, then began gathering water flasks, saddle bags, weapons, and the bedrolls that were untouched. Kaiden tucked a few plates and utensils into the saddle bags.

"We should bury them," Pierce announced.

"With what?" Kaiden questioned, arms spread to their surroundings. "And if what our young tracker says is true, we do not have an hour to spare digging holes."

"Are we mercenaries now? Like the ones likely responsible for this?" Pierce challenged.

Tiffin watched the discussion continue, a frown wrinkling his face. He could barely keep up with the three, philosophizing about the right course of action.

"Bury them if you must, but I will go on," Tiffin interjected. "If we delay, you may as well dig a hole for my aunt too."

The others quieted instantly, sharing glances.

"After the quest is complete...we will honor them as they require," Kaiden suggested.

With a heavy sigh, the other two knights nodded.

Pierce turned to the victims, held a hand over his heart, and spoke. "May you rest in peace, and may we avenge your untimely end. Thank you for your sacrifice. We will use these tools in your honor and not forget what was given this day."

Chapter 6

The four set off once more, Tiffin scouting against the fading sunlight for any sign that they were on the right path. He paused at the top of a steep hill, scanning for shadows behind the clouds. He sighed sadly, shaking out his hand and blinking away the sun's severity.

Below them, at the center of a shallow valley, he pointed out a burned patch of ground, in the middle of which was a small stone hovel. Most of its roof remained intact, but its chimney was cold.

"There. That has to have been the stiguine's handiwork."

Next to the shack were the burned out remains of what appeared to have been a stable. The feed trough was black but recognizable, and Tiffin wished it had been salvageable so he could care for Gertrude properly. She deserved that. She shivered beneath him, tamping one front foot and shaking her mane.

"Guys, it's getting late, and with bandits on the loose, good ones at that, I think we ought to hole up there," Elias recommended.

"With half the roof missing?" Kaiden countered. "How's

that going to be any safer?"

"Four walls and most of a roof gives us more protection than none."

"Is it safe? It's surrounded by stiguine poison," Tiffin cautioned. "It's the ash that's dangerous, and it's everywhere."

Kaiden scanned the area. "There doesn't seem to be any falling. It's humid," he pointed out.

Pierce's eyes narrowed. "I feel like we need to go there." Without waiting for agreement or dissent, Pierce started downhill, detouring from their course.

Kaiden grabbed his arm. "Wait. How are we going to get inside?"

Shaking off his grip, the darker knight scowled. "We can lay out our bedrolls to cross if we need to. But we should investigate now."

"What's got you so excited?" Elias prodded as he slipped down the hill past Tiffin trailing behind Pierce.

"I have a feeling," the man called back.

"Coming!" Kaiden called, nearly knocking Tiffin over in his haste.

Tiffin stumbled, watching the knights, and hesitated. He knew the perils of the poison. And he knew that the dragon must be close. He looked at the surrounding hills, combing the mountainside and adjacent landscape for caves or any signs of nest large enough to house a dragon. But in the diminished light, he couldn't make out much beyond the house where the knights had redirected themselves.

Bastian had given him eight days to finish his quest and return. He had already been gone two nights. This would be the third. If he found the dragon tomorrow and was lucky enough to retrieve a scale from its hide, he would barely have time to get back before the deadline.

Tiffin guided Gertrude to follow their new friends. So far, they had not led him astray. At first light, he would part ways if he needed to and continue his search on his own.

He was used to the acrid smell of the burned fields, but Tiffin had not anticipated the other odor wafting from the hovel. It was putrid like a latrine and so potent, he expected to hear flies. This was dead carcass smell. There was no way this hovel had been unoccupied when it was burned. Tiffin thought the owners could still be inside, killed by the toxins or burned by the fire.

Pierce's speed increased exponentially as he neared his target, and the other knights lifted their feet to follow.

Gertrude sped up as well, but stopped as they reached the edge of the ring where Pierce stood, dancing from one foot to another as he tried to work out a way inside.

"If we stir up the ash, we're as good as dead," Tiffin protested. "If you lay out bedrolls, you'll fan it into the air." Pierce shook his head. "We have to get in there. Now." He looked to the other two knights for propositions then back at the front door, and Tiffin swore the knight was contemplating how long it would take to run from where they were to the entrance.

"Pierce, I can see what you're thinking. Don't do it," Elias begged.

Kaiden grabbed Pierce's arm with a swift tug. "The kid's right. Come on. Over there! It's a pond, Pierce. Lily pads!"

Pierce strained against his grip. "It's Darius!" he thundered, "I can feel him. We have to go now!"

Kaiden's grip tightened, and he shook his friend. "We're

no good to him dead."

The man's face wrinkled. "What do lily pads have to do with it?" he grumbled.

"We can make a path with them," Kaiden answered gently. He swung a hand toward the ashy circle surrounding the house. "The water will trap the ash on the ground like mud. We can cross safely."

Pierce followed the other man's gaze, and his voice broke, eyes glassy as he looked back to his friends. "Fast. We have to be fast. He's in there. I know it."

Elias and Kaiden broke into a run, barely keeping up with Pierce as they raced toward the water source. Tiffin joined, rushing Gertrude faster and ahead of the others. The knife in his boot was practically singing to him to cut the pads from the top of the water.

Tiffin was on the ground, blade in hand, and in the water up to his shoulders before the adults reached him. He cut the pads from their base, flinging them up to the shore.

Without a word, Kaiden landed beside him, harvesting more and throwing them with the others. Pierce and Elias gathered the slippery greenery in their bedrolls.

Tiffin threw his last pad to shore, while Kaiden collected the last two in the lake and threw them to the other knights.

Pierce lashed the bedrolls full of slimy lily pads to the horse and jerked his head from Tiffin to Gertrude and back.

"Go!" Tiffin yelled. "Go!" He looked to Gertrude, willing her to give him all the speed she had.

Pierce launched himself onto Gertrude's back, and they spirited toward the building as Tiffin and Kaiden slogged back to the muddy edge.

Elias pulled Tiffin free first, and then they reached

together to bring Kaiden to shore. Their clothes sloshed as they set off toward shore, feet squishing against the now slippery grass. By the time they caught up, a single path of lily pads safely bridged the distance to the entrance. The door was flung open, still rocking on its hinges. Gertrude stood a safe distance away nibbling at a patch of grass. The bedrolls of lily pads was unrolled, abandoned outside the deadly, black ring.

Tiffin followed behind the knights, holding an arm against his face to block the open latrine stench emanating from the building. They tiptoed over the slimy path until they breeched the barrier onto solid ground.

Pierce was on his knees in a stinking puddle. Rancid brown liquid was creeping up his breeches toward his thighs. He cradled a frail-looking man with one arm while attempting to force a flask to his lips with the other.

"Darius!" Elias yelled, joining Pierce and squatting beside them. He squeezed the man's hand, rattling the manacles on his wrist.

"He needs food," Pierce choked out as the man in his arms managed to swallow a small sip. "And we have to get rid of the chains."

The man's arms and legs were shackled to bolts in the floor, preventing him from moving more than a few feet in any direction. Tiffin recognized the puddle for human waste and wondered how long this man had been imprisoned to create such a quantity of squalor. The man's cheeks were hollow, lips stretched tightly over them, and his clothes were matted to his body.

Kaiden nearly knocked Tiffin down as he ran out the door to retrieve the saddle bags.

This was the rare etherae who was supposed to brew the potion to heal his aunt. His faith wavered, hope seeming more a miracle now than a certainty. Should he even continue his quest? The man before him could barely lift his head, let alone concoct an incredibly difficult antidote. Would having the ingredients make any difference?

He watched as the three knights tended the etherae, pressing small bits of bread into his mouth, followed by sips of the flask of ale the castle had packed for him. He hadn't grown to like ale yet, and by the looks of it, neither did Darius.

Tiffin turned to the door, listening to the sound of Elias working at the chains. The clanging iron reminded him of home, and he wished his father was here. The restraints would have already disintegrated under his father's strength and skill. Tiffin, however, had nothing to contribute. He was just taking up space.

He turned to the door. Pierce's bedroll full of lily pads was discarded at the doorway, and Tiffin began widening the path, setting the slimy green pads on either side of the first. He overlapped them so that none of the scorched earth was visible. The sound of Gertrude pulling grass out by the roots calmed his mind as he worked, and he glanced in her direction. They had never wandered this far from home before, but for her part, Gertrude did not appear to be bothered. She had fresh grass, water, and Tiffin, and he got the sense that she was enjoying the adventure with him.

Once Tiffin had exhausted the supply of lily pads, he joined the others inside. The chimney was barren. He inspected the pit and the flue, and believing it functional, he set about building a fire. Darius looked like he could use some warmth, and the knights needed the light.

The sun was setting as he heard the last chain break, and Pierce pulled Darius free of the muck.

Tiffin had a warm blaze in the fireplace, and he eased himself into the corner to rest. The space felt crowded. Maybe if he curled into the corner, he wouldn't trip up the knights.

Elias and Kaiden found a bucket in the corner and took turns refilling it as they cleared the muck away from where Darius had been bound and cleaned him up. The stink began to dissipate after the fourth bucket of water, and slowly, the etherae began to look more human. Pierce picked at him even after Kaiden began preparing food, and Elias focused on the remainder of the cleaning.

Tiffin had difficulty believing Darius was as powerful as the knights claimed. His lean frame looked spindly in the firelight, and his dark, wet hair slicked back against his head. Tiffin thought he might have been a wealthy noble from the castle, but not the important figure that was going to save his aunt—and the entire kingdom.

They had been at it for hours before Darius seemed coherent.

"Pierce?" he asked. His voice sounded like he'd been eating gravel.

"Save your strength," Pierce soothed, pressing another bit of bread between his lips.

Darius frowned but chewed. "You found me," he added after swallowing.

"I always said you couldn't hide from me."

Darius chuckled, then coughed, body wracked with the effort. "Gotta be right, don't you?" he accused.

"Of course."

They were quiet again until Kaiden approached with a plate of hot food. Pierce studied it warily before he accepted the offering and held it closer to his friend.

"I'll help you," he suggested.

After catching his breath, Darius shrugged, trying to break free of his friend's embrace. "Okay, okay. Let me up. I'm not dead," he grumbled. "Your wife is liable to flay me alive if she thinks she has to compete for your affection."

Pierce smiled, helping Darius into a sitting position and bracing him against the wall.

"Give me that bread," Darius insisted, snatching the plate from Pierce. He rested it on his lap and began tearing off bites of roll.

They sat, watching him eat, before Elias began quizzing the etherae.

"How did you get here?" he questioned. "We saw the mess in your chambers. It looks like you took a beating."

Darius arched a brow at him and took such a large bite that he could barely close his mouth around it.

Pierce leveled the other man with one look. "Let him be. The man nearly died from starvation."

Darius waved him off once he'd swallowed. "No, he's right. Time is of the essence. After the first dragon attack, I began searching for spells to counteract the sickness I knew would follow. I'd barely gotten started, and a new page brought my dinner. I should've been suspicious."

Darius slowed his chewing and shook his head.

"You know how I get when I'm working. I only eat if I have to, so I had a couple bites and got back to it. I started to get a little bit lost in the text. And by lost, I mean, I was having trouble reading. The next thing I know, the door opens, and two men run in, grabbing me by the arms."

Elias laughed. "They were poorly informed if they thought you'd go quietly."

"Quite right," Darius agreed. "I threw everything I had at them...until I passed out."

"That was nearly two moons ago!" Pierce exclaimed. "Why did no one raise the flag then that you were missing? How did I not know sooner?"

Darius shrugged. "It's no one's fault. It's not uncommon not to see me for days at a time. And you've been busy with the new baby. I hadn't even gotten a chance to come see her. Is she perfect?"

"Arwen," he murmured. "And yes. She is perfect with a perfectly loud set of lungs. I've gotten more sleep coming after you than I did at home."

The adults chuckled softly.

"So, they poisoned your food?" Kaiden clarified.

"Drugged, not poison. It was supposed to keep me from making a fuss. They weren't planning on me being conscious when they came for me, or they'd have sent more men." He stopped to describe them in detail, and Tiffin wondered how he'd remembered all of it.

"I'll track them," Elias insisted.

"They don't matter. It's Rufus behind it all," Darius announced.

The collective gasp furrowed Tiffin's forehead as he listened.

"Who's Rufus?" he asked. The question had slipped out before he realized it, and suddenly, the etherae looked at him for the first time. Even in his weakened state, his scrutiny crawled over Tiffin with tiny fingers of energy that set Tiffin's hairs reaching for the sky.

"Rufus trained with Darius," Pierce explained. "But he died fifteen years ago when the plague passed through."

Tiffin closed his arms around himself under Darius's inspection. The uncomfortable sensation of electricity skulking over his body made him squirm. He broke eye contact, running his hands through his hair to shake the feeling that he was not alone in his head.

"Who is this?" Darius questioned.

"This is Tiffin," Elias replied. "We found him on our quest to find you."

"That's convenient," Darius noted.

Tiffin wanted to snarl, but he needed this man. "Nothing about my aunt dying is convenient," he snapped.

Darius's expression shifted from sour to guilty in one blink.

Elias tapped Darius's foot with his own. "He checks out. His supplies are definitely from the castle, and he knows all about the dragon."

"His aunt is companion to the princess," Pierce added.

Darius stared Tiffin down. "Tell me everything," he ordered. He passed the remainder of his plate to Pierce, who wasted no time cleaning it.

Tiffin's chin jutted up as he spilled the details. "It's a stiguine. I need one of its scales so you can make the cure."

Darius stared at him. "How do you know it's a stiguine and not a veseander? They both are poisonous."

"I've seen it," Tiffin confirmed. "It killed my friend's cow. I'm not even sure it saw us. It was purely hungry, and it didn't breathe fire or anything. It has scales. Veseanders are smooth. They have dry skin, but not scales. And a veseander is too small to burn those fields as fast as it happened."

Darius arched a brow. "Can't argue with that."

Tiffin told him everything he knew from finding his aunt up to the moment he leaped on his horse and rode out. "But I saw something weird when it attacked the cow. There was a red stone, sort of glowing, on his neck." He touched the hollow of his throat to indicate the position on the dragon.

"I should have guessed," Darius murmured. "It's being controlled. By Rufus."

"Rufus is dead, Darius. We went to his funeral," Pierce reminded.

"All we saw was a wrapped body on fire. It could have been anyone," Darius countered. "I'm not guessing; I know he did this. I've seen him with my own eyes. He left me here about a fortnight ago and hasn't been back since."

"How did you survive without food or water?" Kaiden questioned.

Darius jiggled his head toward the bucket. "It rained. There's a hole in the roof. I got lucky. But you got here just in time."

"There's something else," Elias added. "Earlier today we found a group of men. Dead. Throats slit. I don't think we're alone out here."

"Great," Darius complained. He was still for a bit, hands in his lap. "I haven't heard anyone for a while. Can you describe them?"

Elias gave a well-detailed description of their body types, height, hair color, and any distinguishing marks. Tiffin hadn't gleaned a tenth of the knowledge that he had, and he studied the four men as they strategized.

"As rough as it is, I think our best odds are to stay here for the night, even surrounded by the dragon's ash," Elias suggested.

"I agree," Darius stated. "Tomorrow, we will go where Tiffin believes the dragon is nesting." He turned his eyes on Tiffin resolutely and nodded. "And we will get your scales and return. I can create the cure. The moment we get back to my quarters, I can begin."

Tiffin relaxed at the promise coming from a man who had endured so much so recently.

"We should sleep while we are warm. We will need our strength," Darius cautioned. "Acquiring scales is harder than it sounds."

Tiffin met the other man's eyes. "There were stables here before the fire. In the morning, I will look for any wandering horses. We've only got the one for five of us. We could travel much faster with even one more." Tiffin worried if they didn't find at least one more, that he'd have to give Darius the use of Gertrude.

"The boy is right. I don't know if you'll be able to walk for a while," Pierce added.

Darius grumbled slowly, waving him off.

"I'm serious, Darius. You were on the brink barely an hour ago."

"It was at least three," Darius argued.

Pierce rolled his eyes. "Quit being stubborn. If we can find some horses, this will all go better."

"And where are your horses?" Darius inquired.

"We're not talking about that," Elias mumbled.

"Oh, we're talking about it." Kaiden laughed. "But maybe it'll be better in the morning while we're traveling.

We'll need some entertainment."

"Fair enough." He looked at the others then. "By the way, how did you get inside safely?" Darius questioned. "Rufus forced the dragon to burn the grounds for a long while before he left me for dead. Thought I was going to roast too or just choke on the smoke, but I suppose that was too much to hope for."

"Lily pads," Kaiden explained. "There's a pond nearby. I guess for the horses. We pulled the pads out and covered the ash."

"Smart," Darius approved. "Okay. I'm about to pass out. I suggest you do the same."

True to his word, Darius's eyes closed, and he was unconscious.

"He's in no shape to travel," Elias whispered.

"You know he won't let us go without him," Kaiden disputed.

Pierce shook his head, leaning in and punching a finger against the floor. "I will not let him kill himself. We need to take him back now. Tiffin can finish his mission. Elias, Kaiden, you stay with him, but we find a horse, and I'm taking him back. He can't perform this casting in this shape. He could barely hold his head up. If Tiffin's aunt has any chance of surviving, we have to get him home and healing."

Tiffin frowned. "You can't protect him by yourself. Can he even ride?"

Elias tilted his head in Tiffin's direction. "He's not wrong."

"Look, let's wait till morning," Kaiden advised. "He already looks better. Even if he is sleeping."

"I'll take first watch," Elias offered.

There was no more discussion before they settled down to sleep. Tiffin woke when Elias asked Kaiden to take over and again when Kaiden nudged Pierce awake. Knowing there was no more sleep for him in this cabin, he slipped out the door to search for Gertrude and, hopefully, at least four other horses. It was a lot to ask for, but Tiffin held out hope anyway.

Chapter 7

The sky had turned orange and yellow by the time Tiffin located additional horses. He found two grazing side by side in full gear. He had hoped for three, but it was more than they'd had before, and he led the creatures to the lily pad path in front of the hovel.

They seemed to know the way. He detected a sadness in their cadence, and he realized that whoever had lived here had been good to these animals, and they knew what had happened. They must have been saddled in an effort to escape, but Rufus had seen to it that the owners hadn't survived.

He stroked each horse in turn and decided to find a treat for each. Maybe carrots had escaped in his saddle bags.

He started for the entrance, surprised to find Darius in the doorway, one hand braced on its frame.

"Ah, I see you found Marion and Lawrence," Darius greeted. His mouth quirked in a half smile.

Pierce appeared at his side, propping him up and leading him toward Tiffin. "Great! Horses! And even better—saddles. Can you ride?" he asked the etherae.

"We're about to find out," Darius replied with a smile. He was slow, but the man climbed gingerly onto the steed and took a deep breath as he settled into the saddle. He gripped the saddle's horn tightly, wobbling slightly.

"Maybe we can save the racing till this afternoon," he teased.

Tiffin dipped his head in understanding, unable to think of another response. This mirth seemed very out of place for finding him mostly dead the night before.

Darius turned to him, reins in hand. "I believe your dragon is north of here. It sounded that way after it burned the border around my abode."

"While I was searching for the horses this morning, I thought I saw what could be a cave...or maybe a shadow." Tiffin pointed to a spot about halfway up the mountain.

Squinting, Darius followed his finger. "Good a place as any to start." He looked to his companions. "Where's Kaiden?"

Kaiden came bounding out of the house with the saddle bags slung over his shoulder, his large hands full. He started with Darius, then Tiffin, and finally Elias and Pierce.

Tiffin looked down at the warm offering, seeing something gooey inside the bread, and something green that looked like chopped grass. He sniffed it tentatively and was shocked when his mouth watered. He took a bite, the bread warm and softer than he expected. Its crust crackled under his teeth, and he recognized the flavor of cheese and something savory, almost like onions, mixed in, and he chewed slowly.

"I'll stay with Darius," Pierce announced, one hand on the horse Darius was astride. "Kaiden, you take the first ride.

Elias, if you'll scout ahead, that would be great."

Elias nodded, darting into the lead. When Darius jiggled the reins on Marion, all the horses started forward, Gertrude included.

Tiffin was practically chafing on Gertrude's back to run for the dragon's nest. He took his time eating instead as she trotted with the pack. He sighed sadly as he swallowed the last bite, licking his fingers. His aunt would be disappointed in his behavior, and he wiped the remainder discreetly on the leg of his breeches instead.

Darius was keeping pace with him, and Tiffin glanced at him every few moments.

"I sense you have questions. Ask them," Darius encouraged. "A curious mind is a healthy mind."

Tiffin worried his lower lip as they rode, formulating a question. "How is this Rufus connected with the dragon?"

Darius sighed. "Rufus and I trained together when we were even younger than you. Rufus is an exceptionally talented etherae. He worked harder than anyone else in our class, myself included. However, he could never outdo me. He tried, though." The etherae wagged a finger in the air. "And, like a fool, I took the bait. Every time he challenged me." He shook his head.

"He doesn't sound like a very good man."

Darius shrugged. "Good and bad are two sides of the same coin," he reasoned. "I should have given him more sympathy. As skilled as Rufus became, he has almost no natural talent. And he was dabbling in some very unnatural arts. Syphoning power. Mind control. Necromancy. While unethical, they all require an incredible amount of knowledge and skill to perform."

Tiffin shivered at the thought. "Why does anyone turn to those things?"

"Power," Darius answered quickly then shook his head. "It's all very alluring: the ability to gain power by thwarting your enemies, making someone do all your chores so you can take a nap, bringing someone you love back from the dead." He cast a sidelong glance at Tiffin. "It's almost understandable."

"But it's an affront to nature," Tiffin countered, remembering the dull philosophy lessons with the princess. "It removes things from the natural order."

Darius arched a brow. "For a boy without training, you are well versed in the ethos of the etherae."

"I know the creed," Tiffin replied. "Doesn't practicing the unnatural arts alter an etherae? Discarding the tenets of the creed will lead one to false conclusions."

Darius smiled. "How did you learn this?"

Tiffin looked away, clearing his throat. "My aunt is the princess's companion. Since I was about five, she's been sneaking me into the castle to overhear the lessons from a hiding spot."

"I'm impressed with your ingenuity."

"It was all Aunt Helen. I hate philosophy. It's so boring."

"But critical in learning about the world and how to avoid mistreatment or mistreating others," Darius added.

"Did Rufus not receive these same lessons? And yet, you did not have the same outcome," Tiffin pointed out.

Darius nodded. "As I said, he wants power, and he wants to be right. If you told Rufus something was too difficult, he'd pursue it to prove it could be done. He lost sight in his right eye proving a point once." He paused again as the horses shifted their gait to match the upward slope of the terrain, and Darius gripped the reins, face contorting with pain.

Pierce placed a hand on his calf, guiding the horse and ensuring his friend's placement.

Tiffin watched the exchange. "And how long have you known Pierce?"

He laughed. "Since I first came to the castle. That was two decades ago. I met the three of them over a pint of ale, and the four of us have been thick as thieves ever since. But they have wives and children now. And I'm godfather to at least two of them. Maybe three. I've started to lose count."

Tiffin chuckled.

"So, you will understand me when I tell you that nothing must happen to them on this quest. Their families are counting on it, and I am not prepared to rear any children in their absence." Darius met his eyes.

His crystal blue gaze was unnerving in its intensity. The words he spoke sounded pleasant, but Tiffin understood their implications.

"You are not prepared to raise children, and I am not prepared to let my aunt die. Bastian said I have eight days. We have already used half of them to get here, and I haven't found the dragon yet. Once we get the scale, we still need to ride back with enough time to cure her."

Darius didn't answer for a moment as they navigated a narrow pathway, allowing Tiffin to lead them until the road widened, and he nudged his horse next to Gertrude. "I am sorry that you were sent alone on this mission. It's good that you happened upon my friends when you did."

Tiffin stiffened at the suggestion that he wasn't capable of doing this task alone. "They were fortunate to have stumbled on me. They were cold and without supplies."

Darius snorted. "I heard about the card game. You are not afraid to paint a picture exactly as it is," he surmised. They rode a few more paces. "Before we get the scales, Tiffin, it is imperative that we remove the stone from the dragon's neck. Rufus is using it to control him. Stiguine wouldn't burn fields without being compelled."

"Okay, but how are we supposed to do that?"

"We'll assess the situation when we find the dragon and make a plan at that time. But if we don't get the amulet off, we'll stand no chance of getting what we need for the cure. Rufus won't allow it, and the stiguine will keep terrorizing the lands. All the cure in the world won't help."

Tiffin considered his words. He didn't see how they would accomplish what needed to be done. They were three knights, a boy, and an etherae recovering from starvation who couldn't walk without help. Against a stiguine.

"Bastian suggested that we sneak in while it's sleeping and pull one out," Tiffin explained.

Darius laughed. "That is because Bastian has no idea the size of these scales. It's not like a fish where you could fit them on the tip of your finger. They're bigger than your head."

"You've seen one before?"

"Only in books. There are less than five known cases of anyone surviving stiguine poison. And it was a long time ago. Stiguines are not as common as they used to be."

"How did they do it back then?"

"It took an army of men to slay it. But the account is vague on how they accomplished that. I've read it many times. I've always thought it might be embellished, and they simply found one dead of old age or else slayed a newborn."

Tiffin hadn't ever considered a newborn stiguine dragon. No one knew how long they lived for certain, but it was thought to be a longer span than for men.

Shortly before midday, the pungent smell of sulfur and methane filled the air. Tiffin covered his nose with his sleeve and strained his ear toward the cave. "I think I hear him breathing."

Darius nodded. "He's a big one. Full belly, too."

Tiffin wrinkled his nose, trying not to choke on the smell. "It's getting stronger as we get closer."

Kaiden eased off the horse's back. "I can fix that," he offered. He darted into the forest, leaving the others to stare at each other with shrugs.

Elias hopped up on the horse. "If he thinks he's getting this back, he's wrong." He grabbed the reins and pranced about, wiggling his toes.

When Kaiden returned, his grin stretched from ear to ear. He held up both hands, green vines dangling haphazardly between his fingers.

"Whatcha got there?" Pierce asked.

"Herbs. Wrap these babies up in a bit of cloth and throw it over your nose. It'll smell better than dragon farts."

For all the time Tiffin had spent thinking about dragons, he had never once thought about them farting. He burst out laughing as he imagined it, covering his mouth with his hand, trying to get a grip on himself as Gertrude snorted beneath him. His heavy heart lit up with the silly thought, and some of the tension released from his shoulders.

Darius leaned forward in his saddle with a grin. "You're picturing trees bending in the wind, aren't you?" he questioned.

"Yes," Tiffin croaked and laid his head on Gertrude's neck, tears rolling down his cheeks. His body shook, and when he finally sat back up, Kaiden passed him a cloth to tie around his nose and mouth. Immediately, he smelled mint and something sweet that he couldn't place. It was a drastic improvement over the brimstone he'd been smelling all day.

"Let's get on with this," Elias prompted.

The troop marched forward, Darius picking up the pace as they approached the cavern. Gertrude sped up giddily. When they were close enough, they dismounted, Pierce grunting as he rushed to help Darius from his horse.

"I've got it," Darius shushed. "I'm getting stronger all the time. I'm not an invalid."

Pierce growled. "There is no shame in admitting you're weak. It's temporary, I know. But if you get stubborn and hurt yourself, then what are we supposed to do? Rufus will kill us all and mount your head on a spike to show everyone he beat you."

Darius brushed his friend off, straightening up and looking at Tiffin. "Let's..." He glanced away as Elias and Kaiden whizzed by them in a half crouch toward the lair.

Tiffin slipped off Gertrude, pulling his sword free of the pack. With a nod to the etherae and the knight, he darted after the others, catching up quickly. As they were about to crest the hill, Elias motioned for them to stop.

Tiffin could see the tip of the stiguine's tail and heard the rhythmic breathing of a creature asleep. Up close, he could see the size of the scales near the tip of its tail. The tiny ones were the size of his head. As he looked up its body toward its head, the scales grew larger as they neared its belly.

Tiffin's brain was whirling. He wondered if he could simply walk up, pull one off its tail and run home. A hand dropped onto his shoulder, and he twisted to see Darius behind him shaking his head.

The etherae touched the hollow of his throat then glanced at the animal.

Remembering Darius's words about removing the stone first, Tiffin looked past his companions at the large rocks and boulders lining the cave's edge. Each was bigger than Gertrude, and it looked like they'd been shoved aside to make room for the beast. Deep claw marks covered their bases, flat from the friction of being pushed.

He eased forward, timing his footsteps with the dragon's exhalations. It felt like ages walking the length of the beast, but he pressed forward until he could see the red stone where its neck met the trunk of its body. Now that he was within a dozen feet of it, the red pulsing stone was much larger than his aunt's stew pot. A silhouette of a figure inside the stone moved, and Tiffin ducked behind the nearest boulder to hide.

Darius crept toward him, pressing beside him behind the large rock. He held a shushing finger to his lips then peeked around their cover to study the stone.

Tiffin watched him closely, peering around the other corner of the rock he was hiding behind to see what he could make out. The red stone did not appear to be pulsing. It was more like a giant, smooth ruby. The cave was dark, and the dragon's nostrils glowed as it exhaled, one foot twitching in its sleep. The solitary other light emanated from the depth of the stone at its neck, but it was unwavering upon closer inspection.

Darius reached for the tie at his waist, unknotting it with shaky fingers. He pulled it free then tugged at the bottom of his shirt and lifted it over his head.

Tiffin's brow scrunched. He wanted to whisper, but he had no knowledge of the hearing abilities of a beast the size of the one a dozen feet away. He assumed that bigger ears came with bigger hearing. He watched the shirtless etherae, his ribs protruding from beneath his taut skin. Darius dropped into a crouch, adjusting the cloth between his hands. He shifted his weight silently from one leg to the other. Tiffin didn't know where the strength to hold the position or move quickly had come from, but he attributed it to herbs that Kaiden must have put in their food.

Pierce grabbed at Darius, but it was too late. Crouched low to the ground, Darius was half-way to the sleeping stiguine in an instant. His feet slipped silently across the ground till he reached the dragon's throat and wrapped his shirt around the stone. He twisted it gently, then froze as the dragon snorted, undulating its neck. Darius tripped, losing his grip, and caught himself on his hands as he hit the floor.

Pierce leaped away from the safety of the boulders, armor clanking as he skidded in front of his friend and wrapped himself around the other man.

Tiffin's body started to launch toward the danger, but he stopped as the dragon stirred, its colossal purple eyes snapping open at the sound. The ground rumbled beneath them as the creature rolled from its side to its feet. Its purple iris flicked across the cave.

Pierce pulled Darius toward the rocks, and Elias and Kaiden jumped in front of them, swords bared in a defensive position.

The dragon shook itself back to consciousness. It didn't appear angry yet, merely startled and checking for danger. Its gargantuan nostrils, nearly the size of Tiffin himself, snuffled at the ground.

He considered throwing his mask of herbs in front of it to make the stiguine sneeze and buy them time. However, if it breathed fire, they'd all be roasted like pigs. He had to think of something. He needed that scale. Aunt Helen was counting on it.

Chapter 8

Tiffin jumped out from behind his cover in the opposite direction of the knights, throwing his hands over his head, eyes downcast, and held his ground. He needed to show the dragon that it had nothing to fear from him.

The others gasped, whispering for him to get back and demanding to know what he was doing. He ignored them, deciding to treat the creature like a horse. It was an animal after all, and all he had to do was show that he was there to help and not harm.

The first time he'd shoed Gertrude, he'd barely stood tall enough to reach her shoulder. But she had eased into trust as he moved slowly and confidently. He had to let Gertrude come to him. The stiguine would need to trust him too if he was going to retrieve the amulet and get the scale.

The creature sniffed the air as it zeroed in on him. Dust and bits of crushed stone puffed around his knees with each exhaled breath. Cool air from outside the cave rushed around him with each inhale, and he concentrated on not shivering at the change in temperature.

He took a few deep breaths himself, drawing on the confidence he used when he was talking to horses he didn't know.

"Good morning," he murmured soothingly. "You were having a good sleep."

He knew it didn't matter what he said as long as his tone conveyed his intentions. He placed his palm against the base of his throat.

"Who put this on you, buddy?" he asked softly, braving another step closer to the animal's throat. Slowly, he extended his hand toward the base of the dragon's throat, hoping it understood the connection.

The dragon's neck rolled around the tight space, adjusting until its face leveled with his, chin brushing the ground. Up close, even the sweetly scented herbs Kaiden had prepared couldn't abate the sulfur that dried every inch of his skin in an instant. He had never been so hot before and unable to sweat.

Tiffin touched his throat again. "I need to take it off you," he explained. "But I promise not to hurt you. You'll feel better once it's gone. Would you let me do that for you?"

The stiguine's nostrils flared, lips curling upward to bare its teeth. Its upper lip rippled, and a low growl emanated from its mouth. Its purple eyes turned to slits as its head edged closer.

He blinked, freezing in position again briefly. He held both hands up to the creature, palms out and fingers spread to indicate he had no weapons.

The dragon sniffed again, so close to his hands that Tiffin swore he felt its muzzle touching him. The excitement of not having been eaten already dissipated as something gooey and warm like congealed oatmeal coated his hands and the top of his head. He cringed, stomach roiling, and he swallowed back the desire to vomit.

A warm glob rolled down his nose, landing with splat near his feet. He heard gagging from behind the rocks. His gaze flicked to the dragon's eyes which were already rolling toward the noise.

With gut wrenching boldness, Tiffin scooped a trail of slime from the side of his face and let it plop to the ground. It splattered up onto his calves. He reached to swipe another glob from his hair and tossed it down.

"You'd better hope this washes out, or Aunt Helen will come give you a piece of her mind," Tiffin sassed gently.

His commentary had the desired effect, drawing the creature's focus. It only had purple eyes for him.

He gulped and stepped closer to the dragon. Keeping one hand over his head in supplication, he inched sideways toward the amulet.

The dragon blinked, and its upper lip slowly covered its yellowed teeth, face lowering less than a foot from the ground. It was relaxing.

This time, Tiffin took a bigger step closer to the amulet, where Darius's ragged shirt miraculously clung.

He looked into the dragon's eyes, mesmerized by the patterns flowing through the irises.

"Get the amulet," Darius urged in a whisper.

The stiguine's gaze shifted suddenly, searching for the source of the voice.

"I'm right here," Tiffin stated, his words a bit louder. He needed the dragon to watch him. Needed it to make no mistake that he was here to free it, not enslave it. He wiggled the fingers of his hand in the air until he felt the dragon's eyes turn back to him.

Tiffin noticed the ridges on the top of the dragon's head as they pulsed gently like a long shiver that began above its eyebrows, down the back of its neck, over its shoulders, and he assumed all the way to its tail. But Tiffin didn't bother to check. He had to get to the amulet. Part of him wished he could have happened upon this dragon at some other time when he could try to befriend it.

He took another step and another, the dragon's head following a foot away. He held his breath as his fingers made contact with the stone. A red glow pulsed through the homespun weave, brighter at first and then fading, and Tiffin gulped.

Time was running out, and he closed the remaining distance. The dragon would either kill him or let him live, but he didn't have the time to waste worrying which it was going to be. His other hand closed around it, fingertips slipping closer and closer to the dragon's skin. The stone was smooth and warm, distracting him as he searched out how it was bound to the animal.

Finding the bail at the top of the pendant, he worked his fingertips up to a wire. The metal was rough, pricking Tiffin's fingers as he sought a clasp. The flesh around it was raised and wet, and he did his best not to touch the sensitive spots.

"Oh, poor thing," he murmured.

Pulling back, he squirmed to get a look beneath the scales and squinted as he examined the infected flesh starting to wrap around the wire. He couldn't lift it over the creature's head. Maybe he could cut it if he had the right tool. Maybe the knife in his boot would do the trick. He was quite sure that if he pulled a knife out, the dragon would snap him in half before he'd even made the attempt.

The dragon's breathing was growing shallow as Tiffin worked. Finally, he slipped both hands beneath the scales till he found the fastening. The metal was wet with blood or worse, but he finally felt a simple hook and eyelet clasp. He would have to squeeze the two together to release it. It was going to hurt.

"Oh, buddy, I'm so sorry." He felt his voice cracking as he spoke. He wasn't sure how to soothe the great animal. "I'm going to take this off," he explained, looking at its eyes again. "Give me a moment."

He leaned in, pressing his cheek to the animal's neck, locking their gazes. "I'm right here with you. Right here. I'll be quick."

Its scales were shockingly cool to the touch in comparison to the heat beneath them. He focused his attention, wrapping one hand around the hook and the other around the eye. Tiffin took a deep breath, allowing the creature to feel it through his cheek. He released the air from his lungs over eight counts.

His grip was firm, and with all his strength, he squeezed the two ends together.

The stiguine's neck jutted to the opposite end of the cavern before it stiffened as it began to screech in pain.

However, as its neck lengthened, the metal shifted beneath Tiffin's grasp, making room for the two ends to uncouple. He gasped in relief as the tension immediately eased. He had done it!

The victory was short lived as the weight of the amulet pulled at the wire in his hands. It was slick with blood and puss, and Tiffin fumbled.

He scrambled to catch it, hands clapping together clumsily as it passed between his palms. An empty slap filled the air, and Tiffin knew what would come next. The stone was going to shatter, and who knew what power would be released when it did.

He squeezed his eyes shut so he wouldn't have to see it hit the ground. Tiffin imagined it would create a massive explosion that would turn them to oozy splatter against the walls. And if it by some chance didn't explode, the dragon might be startled and treat itself to a tasty snack. His braced for impact, his whole body puckering into itself, covering his head beneath his elbows, one knee drawing up to protect his belly, the other knee dropping him to the ground until he resembled a twisted ball of flesh. Heartbeat thrumming against his eardrums, Tiffin waited for the sound of breaking glass, and he pressed himself backwards until there was nowhere else to go but into the dragon's hide.

The dragon's cry ceased followed by panting. Tiffin could feel its rapid breaths against his back. He pulled one hand away from his face to look over his shoulder where he had pressed himself into the fold of the dragon's front leg at the trunk of its body. He was in its armpit!

Where was the amulet? How was he still breathing? Catching a twitch in front of him, he found Elias, belly to the ground, arms outstretched. Between his palms rested the stone tangled in Darius's shirt.

They blinked at each other, afraid to speak.

The dragon's neck began to swirl again as its breathing evened, and Tiffin recoiled as its nose abutted his chest, grateful for the chain mail separating them. He held his breath, staring into the animal's eyes and slowly unclenched his fists, holding them palm out again.

Under normal circumstances, Elias's whimper would have gone unheard, but in the abrupt silence, it sounded like a lightning strike, echoing off the hard walls.

Slowly, the stiguine's head floated down and sniffed at Elias's prone form. Its body shifted, feet rolling calmly until it was once more belly to the ground. The great head rested on the floor then, staring but unthreatening.

"That has to feel better," Tiffin soothed. He smiled, again, not showing his teeth, then crouched down to the prostrated knight. "Get up," he whispered to Elias.

The olive-skinned man glanced up at him, drew the stone to his chest, and rose to his feet smoothly. He backed away behind the rocks to join his companions.

Darius relieved him of the stone, wrapping it up carefully and passing it to Pierce. He moved toward Tiffin, knees bent, and glanced between Tiffin and the dragon.

"You will need to ask it for the scales. They are similarly attached to its body as hair is to your head," he instructed.

Tiffin blinked. Ask the dragon? Did the dragon speak? It hadn't so far.

Darius nodded encouragingly, backing away a few steps and dropping to one knee.

"U-um," Tiffin stuttered. He looked at his feet and then the dragon's side and finally met his eyes. "I...was hoping I might have one of your scales so this etherae here," he gestured toward Darius, "can heal my aunt. She was poisoned by the ash after you burned our fields."

The dragon made no motion that it understood besides the blink of one eye. The tips of its lips quivered as it blew out a tiny puff of air.

Tiffin waited, glancing at the etherae.

Darius held up a hand, indicating he should be patient, and he looked back at the creature's face. His instinct was to reach for a scale and hold it until it granted permission. He looked to the etherae who knelt silently, head bowed.

Closing his hands together in front of himself, Tiffin mimicked the other man's posture, dropping to one knee and bowing his head. He concentrated on his breathing, making it slow and even as he remained still.

The dragon's vast muzzle pushed Tiffin aside as it tucked its face into its belly. Its flank twitch before its neck swished the opposite direction, stopping when its mouth reached Tiffin.

Between its teeth were two scales, each one the size of serving trays.

"Two?" Tiffin questioned, a tear rolling down his cheek. He could not fail with two! "Thank you." He positioned both arms beneath them, and the stiguine released its grip.

His knees buckled under the weight, and he clasped them to himself. They reminded him of oblong fish scales, and he spotted purple liquid along the flat side of each where they had been withdrawn from its body...dragon blood.

"Thank you," he repeated. "If you ever have need for help, I am at your service."

He had done it. With plenty of help. But he had completed his quest. Overwhelmed, Tiffin swallowed back sobs at the gesture. He dipped his head at the dragon, hoping to convey his gratefulness. He nearly dropped the scales when the dragon dipped its head and closed its eyes briefly before sighing and flopping back to the ground.

Slowly, he backed out of the cave. From the corner of his eye, he saw the others sneaking out from behind the barricade of stone. He concentrated on maintaining his stride and not tripping over anything like a dragon toe or tail on his way out.

"Don't walk backwards, Tiffin." He could hear his aunt scolding inside his head. With a gulp, he pivoted, scuttling out of the cave as fast as his legs would carry him.

Once out of sight of the cave, Kaiden and Elias relieved him of the burden of the scales. Tiffin nearly collapsed in relief.

"Why are they so heavy?" he murmured.

"Full of liquid," Darius replied. "It's not blood, but it's potent. I believe their poison ferments in the scales until they need it. It not only shields them from direct attacks but also poisons anyone who manages to break the first layer. That's why you need fresh ones. Ones that shed naturally are hollow."

Tiffin's jaw dropped open. "So, it's the liquid inside that makes the cure?"

Darius nodded as they reached the horses, and he took the wrapped amulet from Pierce. He opened the saddle bags, emptying the papers and the last of the salted meat. He placed the amulet inside, stuffing the sleeves of his shirt protectively around it.

"We'll have to empty the other bags for the scales. I don't think we should try to carry them," Darius advised.

Kaiden reached the horses as Tiffin finished emptying the opposite bag. He grunted as he lifted the scale to drop in the bag. "Does that mean we get to eat it all tonight?"

Pierce laughed. "Do you always think with your belly?"

"That's so dumb, it's not worth answering," Kaiden replied, collecting the items Darius had discarded. He bundled them into a bedroll and lashed it to one of the other horses.

"I know we're ready for a victory dance, but I think time is of the essence," Darius began. "I hear there's an aunt that needs saving, and we should make haste."

Tiffin breathed a sigh of relief. His body trembled as he stared at the scale Elias was struggling to deposit into Gertrude's saddle bags. Not only had he completed his task, he had found the etherae who knew how to use it. She had a fighting chance! That is, if he could get back in time.

Once both dragon scales were loaded, Tiffin climbed on Gertrude's back, settling the reins in his hands. He wanted to offer to ride ahead, but without Darius, his early arrival made no difference.

"We can make it to the base of the mountain by nightfall if we start now," Elias encouraged. "And at the risk of wearing out the horses, I think we can double up. These two are still pretty fresh." He gestured to the pair Tiffin had found near Darius's prison.

"I'll ride with Darius if you don't mind sharing that horse," Pierce offered.

Kaiden and Elias exchanged looks with the others. "This never happened," Kaiden announced. "And you ride in front." He pointed at Elias.

Rolling his eyes, Elias mounted the horse quickly, reaching a hand down to his friend. "Let's go," he insisted.

They went slowly at first, allowing the horses to adjust to their much heavier loads, picking up speed when they found a clearing, and breaking at the first hint that the sun was beginning its final descent into the western horizon.

They camped at a green area near the river, completely unburdening the horses, and set up camp for the night. Kaiden was virtually bouncing with glee while Elias built a fire. Pierce and Darius went to wash themselves in the river, complaining about each other's smell until Tiffin couldn't hear them any longer.

"That was impressive," Elias complimented as the fire sizzled beneath the pot Kaiden had situated over it. "I thought sure that beast was going to have you for lunch and pick its teeth with your bones."

"And then realize *we* would make a tasty dessert," Kaiden added with a laugh.

Tiffin shrugged. "I had to do it. Aunt Helen's counting on me. Dad, too."

"And the whole realm, not to put you under any pressure," Elias added.

Grinning, Tiffin leaned back comfortably on his bedroll. He was deathly tired, smelled like dragon farts, and thought he would have to wash before he saw her again. But in the moment, the salted meat was beginning to smell divine, and he simply wanted to stare at the sky as the daylight faded.

"I couldn't have done it without you. The way you caught that amulet, Elias—I thought sure it would shatter into a thousand pieces and wedge itself into my shins. And then blow up the cave."

Elias beamed at him. "I'm just that good. I leveled up my speed recently, and none too soon, it looks like."

"How do you level up your speed?" Tiffin questioned.

Kaiden, Elias, and Tiffin passed the time discussing etherae training, sharing with Tiffin the best and worst parts about it. They looked up as Darius and Pierce returned, wet headed but dramatically cleaner.

Tiffin squeaked when he realized both had their hands in the air, a knife to their throats, and a dirty stranger pressed to their backs.

Elias and Kaiden were instantly on their feet, swords drawn. Tiffin was a few beats behind them, wielding his weapon with intent.

"Not so fast," the man behind Darius warned. "Why don't you three drop your weapons and back away."

Tiffin eyed the strangers. The one behind Pierce was taller and thin, but wiry. He was dressed in layers of clothing, gone crusty around the edges. Tiffin suddenly understood why his aunt was always after him to clean up.

He shifted his grip on the sword's hilt, struggling to keep it light and lose. He was ready to fight as long as it didn't take too long. They had places to be, and food was on the horizon.

Kaiden laughed, body going limp with amusement. "We're three against two," he taunted. "Why would we give up?"

The man behind Pierce laughed. "Two and a half at best," he retorted. "And that one," he gestured to Darius, "is too important to risk. My man Tiger here loves blood."

The bald man holding Darius hostage nodded, running his tongue near the blade on the etherae's neck. A thin line of blood ran down his neck.

Tiffin's courage solidified. There was too much at stake. He wouldn't be bullied. And he wouldn't let his family down by valuing his own safety above Darius'. As long as Darius survived the encounter, Helen would live.

The bald man tittered maniacally and gestured toward Tiffin. "That one has no stomach for it. He's still a baby. Are you even shaving yet?"

Tiffin bristled at the insult, adjusting his grip and biting his tongue. The knights weren't attacking over words or bantering, and he determined to follow their lead.

"What do you want?" Pierce asked boldly.

"Him," the grungy man replied easily, pointing at Darius.

"Not going to happen," Elias replied, eyes focused on the knife at Pierce's throat.

"Sure it will," tall-and-wiry answered. "And those dragon scales."

"I don't know what you're talking about," Elias denied, not breaking his stance.

"We saw the whole exchange. This boy forcing a reward from the dragon. I really thought it was going to eat you. This one was supposed to die in that cabin. And then you four wandered along and messed up everything."

"We're really good at that," Kaiden countered, his mouth quirking in a defiant grin. "I think there's a level for that."

"You're amused?" the bald man asked.

"A little, yeah. You clearly do not know who you're tangling with," Kaiden replied. "Or you would choose your words more carefully."

Elias was a blur as he swirled toward Darius. He pointed his blade away from the pair and slammed his fist, hilt and all, into the man's nose.

Blood spurted everywhere, and the assailant stumbled backwards, grasping his face. "What was that?" the bald man grumbled.

"You said you like blood," Elias goaded.

Kaiden had wasted no time, pulling Darius free before the verbal assault had ended.

The bloodied nose was all the distraction Pierce needed to whirl and disarm his captor, nearly breaking the other man's wrist in the process.

Tiffin watched the skirmish helplessly, unsure where to insert himself. He loosened his grip on the hilt of his sword, turning it over and over in his anxious fingers and looking for an opening.

Kaiden deposited Darius at Tiffin's side. "Guard him," he instructed, then darted back into the ruckus near Elias.

Elias was engaged with the bald man, barely having to move to ward off the attack, and Kaiden was laughing as he interjected a smack at their attacker at random intervals.

Darius chuckled beside Tiffin.

"I don't know what to do," Tiffin worried.

Darius patted his shoulder. "Stand down, squire. Your bravery is admirable but not necessary. Elias's combat skills are unmatched. They never stood a chance. This is fun for him."

Pierce's battle was far more arduous. While Pierce's raw strength and brawn made his blows formidable, his captor's lithe frame dodged most of them, twining himself around Pierce like a snake.

His attacker's blow struck Pierce hard in the gut, and the knight doubled over. In the next moment, the wiry man whacked the back of his head, and Pierce went down.

Without a thought, Tiffin jumped into the fray, ignoring Darius calling him back. He thrust his sword wildly at the man who was about to kick Pierce a second time. His blade struck with a sickening squish, and his momentum pushed it clean through the man's left shoulder.

He met the wiry man's shocked brown eyes. They were wide open, his mouth fixed in an O shape. Tiffin hadn't intended to wound the man; he merely wanted him to leave Pierce alone. Blood coursed down the blade of the sword onto the hilt, and Tiffin pulled it free before the dark liquid could touch him. Gore arced across the ground, and Tiffin couldn't look away.

"You little cur!" the tall man spat. "You will pay for this!" In an instant, his long arm had roped Tiffin in by the neck and crushed him against his chest.

The man's elbow was locked firmly under Tiffin's chin, and he was squeezing. Tiffin clawed at the man's arm, trying to dislodge it, but the more he struggled, the more the pressure increased, and he felt his throat being crushed. Airways cut off, Tiffin scrambled with his whole body, trying to kick and claw or bite, but he couldn't gain purchase.

The edges of his vision started to darken, and his whole life flashed before his eyes. He had let everyone down. His aunt. His father. His kingdom. The princess.

Chapter 9

The word "NO!" rang out clearly even through the ringing in Tiffin's ears. He was losing his grip on the man's arm, and then suddenly, the man behind him was gone, the offending arm slipping from his neck.

Tiffin fell first to his knees and then to all fours before tipping over to his side. He gasped for air, choking as it burned the back of his throat. He covered the tender spot with one hand, looking around to see who he should thank for the rescue.

Pierce had regained consciousness. He was still on his back, but one foot was pumping triumphantly in the air, and the lithe attacker was on the ground groaning.

Elias reached a hand down to Tiffin. "You okay?"

Tiffin nodded, even as he was half choking on a breath. He allowed himself to be pulled upright.

Turning, Elias pressed his boot against the man's chest. The wiry attacker was curled into the fetal position, hands covering the front of his trousers.

"Did you really nail him in the family jewels?" Elias questioned with a glance at Pierce.

"They were right there. Low hanging fruit," he rationalized, pushing himself to his feet and dusting off his breeches.

"Nice," Elias complimented.

Elias's boot shifted as he bent down to pick up Tiffin's sword then press on the attacker's wounded shoulder. A blood- curdling scream echoed from the man's throat, and Elias pulled his boot away. He held the sword aloft. "Where did you get this masterpiece?"

The question rang genuine to Tiffin's ears, and he coughed before croaking, "My dad made it."

"When this is all over, you must introduce us. I think I need to be his new best friend," Elias announced. He wiped the blade a few times in the grass before passing it back to Tiffin, hilt first.

"What were you thinking?" Darius accused, drawing closer. "I told you they did not need your intervention." His eyes bore holes into Tiffin's skull.

Shrinking back, Tiffin wrapped his free arm around his midsection. "Pierce was on the ground. I had to do something," he defended.

"Kaiden was right there!" He pointed to where the man was standing a foot away. "He could have protected Pierce."

"Not before he got a boot to the face," Tiffin protested belligerently.

Darius growled. "You took an unnecessary risk. You are so anxious to be a hero that you nearly got yourself killed! And it wouldn't matter if I cured your aunt, because your death might kill her! And then your father would kill us."

Tiffin swallowed uncomfortably. "I will not apologize for trying to help my friends when they're down."

Nostrils flaring, Darius turned away.

"Well, this is all very touching, but it ain't done yet," the bald man grumbled, launching himself into Elias's side.

The olive-skinned man landed with a grunt, then shoved his elbow under the man's chin with enough force that they heard a crack. The bald man fell back, clutching at his throat.

"And stay down," Elias sputtered. He stood over the man. "One more word, and you're getting it in the short and curlies too."

"What are we going to do with these jerks?" Kaiden asked. "This one's bleeding out, and that one's plain stupid."

"It would be wise to know who they are, how they found us, and why they want Darius and the scales," Pierce noted.

"They're with Rufus," Darius replied. "They're the ones that took me from my chambers."

Pierce's eyes narrowed. "Why didn't you say something when they grabbed us at the water's edge?"

"Our odds were better with Elias and Kaiden. I thought it best to comply until we reached camp."

"It was the right move," Elias agreed. "When you're outnumbered, increase your numbers." He had already found rope and was nearly finished hogtying the bald man. He had pulled the cloth from around his neck that was full of herbs and wrapped it around the man's mouth. He turned to the wounded man to give him the same treatment.

"We're going to leave them here?" Tiffin asked. "Shouldn't they be brought to court to face judgment?"

"We have three horses and five riders," Darius pointed out. "You want to add two more bodies, one wounded, and expect to get back in time to save your aunt and anyone else infected?"

Tiffin frowned.

"I know it seems harsh, but harsh living breeds harsh ends," Pierce pointed out. He brushed out the dirt from his shirt as best he could and returned to their makeshift camp to have a seat on one of the large rocks. "Is dinner ready yet?"

Kaiden nodded, moving past Tiffin to resume his work, and stoked the fire. He looked first at Darius, then Pierce.

"If I'd have known you would smell so much better, I'd have begged you to take a bath sooner," Kaiden jibed. "You almost killed my appetite."

"Someone write that down for posterity. Kaiden is always hungry!" Elias teased.

Tiffin looked up as Darius took a seat next to him.

"Aren't you still mad at me for interfering?" Tiffin groused.

Darius nodded. "I am. But we have more pressing issues to discuss. We should talk about what happened with the stiguine." His voice was quiet as the other three continued to throw feigned insults as the food bubbled away.

"Why? Did I do something wrong?" Tiffin worried.

"No. In fact, you did everything right. What you displayed in that cave is something I have never witnessed. I thought the wolf that has been following us was remarkable, but the way the dragon responded to you was extraordinary."

Tiffin turned away from the blue eyes staring him down. "Anyone could have done it," he denied. "I guess I wanted it the most."

"That is untrue. And a boy of your age should be finished with lies," Darius corrected. "Tell me about your parents."

He sighed. "My mom died when I was born, so I never

knew her. My dad is the smithy in our village. He's very good."

"You said he crafted your sword?"

Tiffin nodded.

"Is he a great smithy?" Darius pressed.

Tiffin shrugged. "He does some work for the king."

"You mean for the castle?" Darius clarified.

"No. For the king. In fact," Tiffin paused, pulling the small dagger from his boot. "I am pretty sure he made this for the princess."

Darius looked from the blade to him and back. "And why do you have it?"

Tiffin thought the sun must have slapped him across his face, because his cheeks burned, and he looked away as the etherae took the blade from him. "She gave it to me the night I left. At my aunt's bedside. She wanted me to succeed."

Darius's chuckle was soft, and Tiffin watched from the corner of his eye as the other man inspected the tool. "If this is any indication, he is a stellar smithy."

"He wants me to apprentice with him." Despite his efforts, Tiffin couldn't hide the disgust in his voice.

"That would be a great honor," Darius pointed out.

Tiffin clutched his knees, looking away. Of course this impressive etherae would agree with his father. It was as though every adult in the realm wanted to keep him on that forge.

"But also, a great loss. Foolish even," Darius added softly.

Tiffin's head snapped toward the etherae, and his voice cracked as he sputtered, "What? How? Why?"

The etherae's face was calm as he stated, "You have the

kind of talent to rival the best if you were trained."

"Father says we have responsibilities. I don't have time to play around and earn levels."

Darius shrugged. "Responsibilities and obligations, I certainly understand. But I think I may know some people to help shoulder that burden if your father wouldn't mind. Only while you're training, of course."

Tiffin matched his gaze, jaw agape. "Well, Bastian did offer to mentor me if I succeeded."

"You could do that. Bastian is working with half a dozen individuals. But I was thinking that if you would allow it, I'd advise you in your lessons. Bastian has little knowledge of skills like yours."

Was Darius offering to be his mentor instead of Bastian? Bastian was a high-ranking etherae—he had the gold robes to prove it. But Darius out ranked him. Was he really being given the choice of who would mold him? Was he worthy of the choice? "Where would I even start?"

"Animals, of course. That is where your innate talents lie. However, you can learn other skills. It is wise to begin your instruction by harnessing the powers you were born with. Once you have some experience focusing your intent, you can translate that to other studies."

Tiffin was silent. This was great news. He picked at a loose piece of skin around his thumbnail. "I'd like that," he finally admitted.

He expected Darius to offer more encouragement, but instead, Darius stood and walked toward the fire, joining the banter of the older men and begging for food.

How Kaiden managed to make what had been in his saddle bags taste like something worth eating, Tiffin wasn't sure, but he would bet that it was etheric power. He wondered if he would hone his skills as finely. If his father would allow it.

One thing was certain though, Tiffin thought as he settled down into his bedroll with a full belly. If he didn't save his aunt, he wouldn't *want* to train. Tomorrow, he would ride as far and as fast as he could to get back to her. Even if he had to leave the others behind. He would throw Darius over Gertrude's back if he had to. As he drifted to sleep, he felt the wind soaring beneath his body, arms splayed out to both sides. He was the stiguine. And this time, the creature was soaring for the sheer pleasure of it.

The first thing Tiffin did after waking, was pick his way past their two captives to find the stream and wash himself. He wondered what they would do with the men upon their departure. The last thing they needed was more mouths to feed.

The wolf that had been following along waited for him at the shoreline, slaking its thirst. The water felt like ice against his skin, and he washed quickly before jumping out to dry off. If he rode fast enough, he could see his aunt tonight. Hold her hand and tell her it was going to be okay. He could recount his stiguine encounter and tell her all about finding Darius in that disgusting hovel just to watch her face wrinkle in disgust and shush him.

Tiffin thought he heard heavy footfalls behind him, and he tucked his still damp legs into his breeches, darting glances around to find the intruder. He glanced at the wolf who seemed completely unfazed by the sound. He relaxed, tuning his senses, listening for another sound. He was rewarded by a neigh followed by the unmistakable noise of grass being ripped from the ground. Horses!

The two miscreants who were now hog-tied at camp must have had horses! Tiffin dressed hastily and followed what he heard until he found the source. Two horses in full tack were snacking on the foliage. One looked up at his approach. It was a dark mahogany colored male, and it twitched as it studied Tiffin. The other painted mare didn't bother to look up, chewing on a mouthful of tasty herbs.

With a gentle approach, Tiffin gathered the reins of both animals, noting his wolf slinking into the brush to follow.

When he returned to camp, Kaiden was passing out the remains of dinner.

Pierce looked up at his approach, fumbling his breakfast and barely grabbing it before it hit the ground. "Horses!" he yelled. "Two horses!"

Darius laughed. "Ever articulate," he mocked. "Those must be the bandits' horses."

"Genius," Kaiden announced, passing Tiffin his breakfast. The cheese and bread combination filled him up again, and he wasted no time talking or doing anything other than loading up.

Darius was the first to speak as they worked, kicking dirt into their firepit. "Tiffin and I should ride ahead now that we have the means."

"I don't like it," Pierce contradicted. "Are you strong enough to ride alone?"

Darius rolled his eyes. "I'm dramatically improved."

"That doesn't answer my question," Pierce countered.

"He's right," Elias said. "Getting the scales back without Darius is useless, and I don't think anyone's going to come between this boy and his family."

"But you'll be unprotected," Pierce continued.

Kaiden laughed. "I thought you knew Darius like a brother. He is more powerful at half strength than all of us together."

Elias nodded. "Smaller parties attract less attention."

"Pierce, I know you want to protect me, and your heart is in the right place—" Darius began, but the knight interrupted.

"I don't want to have to tell my daughter that her godfather isn't here because he got impatient and made a foolish mistake," Pierce retorted.

Darius moved closer, touching his friend's shoulder. He looked small next to Pierce, emaciated from his recent trials and half a head shorter. "I will not make you do that," he promised. "You three will have your hands full with those two. Make them walk back. That ought to feel good after being bound all night."

"Are you sure?" Pierce questioned. "I feel like I should be with you."

Darius was firm as he answered. "I know you do. But three to two, you have the advantage. Two versus two, maybe not. But take the second scale with you. I think it wise to divide our spoils in case we find more trouble along the way."

Pierce growled low in his throat, then pushed past Darius to Gertrude. He wrenched the second scale out of the packs, carrying it to his bedroll that was still on the ground, and began wrapping it up.

Darius sighed, turning to the others. "It's settled then. There is still some bread in the pack and if need be, I'm sure we can find something to sustain ourselves. It will give us more impetus not to stop riding till we reach the castle."

Tiffin patted Gertrude's flank affectionately, checking her for burs and securing the remaining scale in the bags. With one last check at their camp, he mounted. "We'd better hurry. Sun's almost all the way up." He cast a glance at Pierce. "I'll take care of him. And don't forget, we've got a wolf with us."

Darius wasted no time pulling himself up onto the dappled mare he had shared with Pierce the day prior, and they set off, building speed as the horses found a sure path leading them home.

They rode for hours, stopping briefly to avail themselves of Kaiden's fine cooking and stretch. Otherwise, they pressed forward like men possessed, with barely a word exchanged between them.

Tiffin wasn't sure where Gertrude found her strength after seven days of hard riding, or how his teeth didn't clatter right out of his head. But his every thought was of the last time he'd seen Aunt Helen. Her skin had been damp, pale, and hot like the forge. She'd looked like a dead body that hadn't quite stopped breathing yet.

And at the thought of her eyelashes fluttering against blue-tinted cheeks, Tiffin urged Gertrude faster and faster. The mare kept pace beside him, and he checked to ensure that Darius was still astride her and not having trouble holding on. He did not look much better than his dying aunt had. But his jaw was clenched in determination, body rising and falling naturally with the horse's gallop. He was an accomplished equestrian too, and if the ride bothered him, he hid it well.

Tiffin hoped it was enough to get them to their destination in time.

Chapter 10

When Gertrude's hooves struck the familiar streets near the castle, they didn't slow, barreling through at a breakneck pace until they reached the gates.

Tiffin and Darius started to fall from their horses as they finally pulled to a stop, but the posted guards caught them in time.

"Master Darius!" one of them yelled. He flagged the others with a wave of his arm.

"Get us to the keep," Darius ordered. "These horses are spent."

"Looks like you are too, master. Rest a moment."

"No time," Darius grunted. His fingers were curled tightly as though still wrapped around the reins, and he grimaced as he tried to flex them. "We have the dragon scale. Take us to my chambers. Now."

The guards stopped arguing, bracing him against their bodies and pulling him through the gates.

With similar assistance, Tiffin gathered Gertrude's reins and led her beside them as they walked.

She neighed relief, and he caught her looking at him.

Spent was the perfect word for her, Tiffin thought. She would recover, but he promised silently to never put her through her paces like this again. He also promised her new shoes and a bath, and all the sweet hay she could stomach. She blew raspberries at him as they walked.

"What about Pierce, Elias, and Kaiden?" Tiffin called forward.

"Yes!" Darius exclaimed, clutching the arm of the man next to him. "The three knights the king sent after me. They are behind us. They have two prisoners. Bring them home."

"But, Master, it's after dark," he protested.

Darius growled. "I hadn't noticed," he grumbled, gesturing at the stars overhead. "Send a cadre to meet them. Go as far as is safe. They have no supplies."

"Did I hear Kaiden is with them? And Elias?" one guard questioned. Given his armor, Tiffin assumed he must be the leader.

When Darius nodded, the guard laughed. "They'll come back fatter than when they left."

Tiffin saw ahead the most beautiful sight he could recall beholding. A small wagon full of hay and crates of something red was hitched to a pair of fresh horses. The guards deposited him and Darius in the back of it.

"The dragon scale!" Darius yelled. "Someone get the scale from the horse."

The guard who had helped him jumped, yanking the milky green object from the pack and setting it gently between them. Then, he leaped into the front seat, grabbing up the reins.

"Hold on!" the guard yelled.

The cart lurched forward, bumping over the street, and

Tiffin watched as another guard led Gertrude away, hopefully for a good grooming and feeding.

Generally, Tiffin didn't like riding in the backs of wagons. They were bumpy and slow compared to horseback. At present, he had never been happier to let someone else control the ride. The hay buffered the majority of the bouncing, and he stretched on his back, staring at the night sky sprinkled with starlight.

"Apples!" Darius pressed one into his hand, and Tiffin needed no encouragement to bite into it.

By the time they reached the keep, Tiffin had gorged himself on four of the fruits. He wiped his sticky fingers on his breeches as they arrived at their destination and reached for the scale.

Darius hooked a finger for him to follow once he had picked it up. "I'm seriously reconsidering why I wanted my quarters to be so far from the rest of the castle," he grumbled.

There were two flights of stairs before they reached his chambers, and Tiffin thought his arms might fall off before he was able to set the heavy scale on the space Darius cleared by swiping his arm across a table. Papers were still fluttering to the ground.

Darius leaned hard against the surface across from Tiffin, who laid the whole upper half of his body over the scale in exhaustion. When he felt a touch on his shoulder, he lifted himself.

"Go to your aunt. I will prepare the potion and bring it to her as soon as it's ready. You have my word."

The gracious side of Tiffin wanted to tell him to rest for at least five minutes, but he didn't know if they had the time. The practical side of him nodded his head.

"Thank you," he mumbled, then shuffled to the door. He eyed the stairs, remembering how many there were, and leaned against the wall for support as one foot slipped in front of the other. Each descending step sent shockwaves up his back. When he reached the last step, Tiffin fell to his backside.

Every bone in his body hurt. It hurt to sit. It hurt to stand. It hurt to walk or touch his own hair. Coupled with worry, Tiffin could do nothing but sob, head on his knees. He smelled the road on his breeches, and the aroma was the same as Gertrude's who hadn't had a bath in a week.

He heard footsteps nearby but didn't bother to lift his head. He wasn't sure he could. His ribs hurt. He had never been this tired before.

A pair of familiar arms wrapped around him, and he recognized the smell of his father's soot-stained clothing. A long, coarse beard scraped against his cheek, and he buried himself in it.

"Tiffin!" His father's voice was full of concern, as his large hands gently lifted Tiffin's face to his. "Son, are you okay?"

The sight of his father's gigantic head evoked a fresh wave of tears, and Tiffin curled against the other man, pressing his head into the crook of his neck.

Aaron stroked Tiffin's head, holding onto him like a vise grip. "Did you get the dragon's scale?"

Tiffin nodded. "Is she alive?"

"Barely. Come on. I'll take you to her."

"I can't. It hurts everywhere, Dad," Tiffin moaned, wiping the tears from his face and trying to press them down into his belly.

"I've got you," Aaron murmured. He scooped Tiffin into his arms, carrying him down the hall like a load of firewood.

Tiffin wrapped his arms around his father's neck, hiding in his massive beard. Maybe he wasn't quite ready to be a man yet. He wanted to be with his dad.

Aaron deposited him gently on the side of the bed where his aunt lay. The mattress was like heaven beneath him. Relieved of some of his pain, he leaned forward to run two fingers over her forehead.

She was cool and dry, and perfectly still. If he stared long enough, he could see her chest rising and falling listlessly. Her hands were crossed over her torso, and Tiffin gulped at the sight.

"Bastian has been tending her every few hours since you left," Aaron expounded. "He's given her potions. He said it would prolong her time so the remedy could be made. The princess has been bringing cool cloths for her to combat the fever."

Tiffin wanted to cry as he sat beside her, but he was out of tears. "I found the grand master etherae that Bastian said could make the potion."

Aaron shook his head, mouth hanging open. "You did? How? Where?"

He turned to his father, recounting the journey he had completed, telling him about the wolf, the knights, and the etherae he had collected.

"And I didn't just get one scale, Dad," he ended. "I got two. The dragon pulled them out itself and put them in my arms. They're so heavy. Darius says they're full of venom or poison or something, which is why they weigh so much. Dragon scales are actually hollow. Or at least, stiguine ones are."

His father nodded. "So, the scale itself is useless? It's the liquid inside that will cure your aunt?"

Tiffin shrugged. "I don't really know. But that's what Darius said."

"Darius is the grand master etherae who's been missing?" he questioned.

"Yes." Tiffin wanted to tell him all about Darius and his offer to undertake his tutelage, but he refrained. Aaron was scrubbing his fingers through his beard, twisting pieces of it, then untangling it. Until Helen was safe, he thought it wise not to ask for favors. He didn't want his father to say no.

"Boy, I'd like to put one over the fireplace once it's been emptied. I want to tell everyone about how brave my son is."

Tiffin rolled his eyes. "Dad, they're like serving trays." He held out his arms to demonstrate the size. "Our fireplace isn't that big."

"You know what I mean. I want everyone to know how brave you are. You are the best thing I ever did, son."

Tiffin looked away. "I only care if Aunt Helen gets better."

He heard his father sigh. "Me too. I'm glad you're home and safe. Why don't you lie down and rest? She won't mind. Are you hungry? I'll get you food."

He was starving but chewing sounded like a lot of work, and his belly was full of apples. "Maybe some soup," he requested. "I'm too tired for anything more. I'll eat later. I've been riding since sunup."

"Yes, of course." His father rose and hurried out of the room.

Tiffin had spent many nights as a boy napping with his

aunt. She usually smelled nice, and he felt safe with her. Now, as he allowed himself to stretch out beside her, one hand on hers, he hoped she felt safe with him.

Tiffin wasn't sure what the hour was when his father's hands lifted him bodily. He startled awake, blinking. Seeing Darius, he scurried out of the way.

The etherae held a small bottle, about the size of an apple, one thumb pressing on the stopper. The liquid inside seemed to be stirring itself, a swirling mixture of milky and dark green. A long glass tube was clutched tightly in his other hand.

"Dad, this is Darius," Tiffin introduced sleepily, rubbing his eyes.

His father nodded once.

"I must warn you," Darius cautioned. "This will be frightening, but please, whatever you do, do not stop me. I assure you that this is normal, and I can explain all after it's over. If I need your help, I will ask."

Darius sat next to Helen on the bed, gently removing the stopper. He stared at her silently, and Tiffin wondered what he was waiting for. They had nearly killed themselves riding to save her, and now, Darius was staring down at her. The etherae tucked her hair behind one ear, two fingers sliding down to her lips. Gently, he pried them apart.

He placed the container and its stopper on the table next to the bed, using the glass tube to draw up the liquid. He slipped his free hand behind her neck to tilt her head back.

The motions reminded Tiffin of the way he might handle a newborn goat. His touch was gentle, and he moved her with great concern, and Tiffin realized how close to death she must be. Darius was focused monomaniacally on his task, as though he and Helen were alone in the room.

Over Helen's parted lips, Darius positioned the tube. The second he removed his thumb from the top, the liquid dropped into her mouth. He eased her head down to the pillow, adjusting her quickly into a comfortable-looking position, grabbed up the container, and darted to the foot of the bed. His eyes glanced between Tiffin and his father.

"Hold fast," he warned. "You won't like the next part."

Tiffin looked expectantly at his aunt. She was unchanged, her lips parted. And then he noticed the smoke rising from her mouth. It was white, curling pungently as it climbed higher and higher. He glanced at Darius who was carefully sealing the bottle and wrapping the tube in a special cloth he drew from his pocket.

The smell that followed reminded him of the fields fallow from the dragon's poison. The odor thickened, and Tiffin covered his nose. If Darius thought the cure was safe, Tiffin trusted him despite the panic coursing through his veins.

"This is normal?" his father barked, kneeling at Helen's side.

"Yes. Get back," Darius yelled. He yanked on Aaron's shoulder in earnest.

Aaron looked like he was about to throw a punch, but he did as instructed and backed up closer to Tiffin.

In the next instant, fire bloomed from her mouth a few feet in the air, and Helen's back arched as she screamed.

Tiffin jumped, grabbing his father's arm to steady them both. The fire spewing from her gullet was blue, and it looked like a geyser. He sighed relief as the flames began to die down after a minute, but the screaming continued. Then, as Tiffin watched in horror, the fires turned purple and began crawling out of her mouth, like a thin sheet across her cheeks, spreading to her whole face and then fanning eventually all over her body.

She was arched like a bridge in the center of the bed, her cries altogether unnatural.

"This is the venom burning itself from her body," Darius explained. "It must leave through her skin. It will not burn her because she is the fuel, but it would burn us," he explained. "We must not give it flesh to feed on."

Aaron dropped to his knees, one hand gripping Tiffin's calf. Tiffin wrapped his arms around his father's head, pulling it to his chest. "Don't look, Dad. It'll be over soon," he soothed.

Darius nodded to him as he folded his hands and bore witness.

Helen's screams died down, and slowly, her back relaxed into the bed. The flames were calming now, waning as they turned green and then sputtering out as quickly as they had spread, leaving her limp.

Darius was at her side in the space of a breath, running his hand over her face, neck, and arms. "It has done its good work. But her body must rest now." He repositioned her arms into the calm pose she had taken before, folding her hands, one atop the other. He pressed his hand over hers.

"That's it? We just... wait and see?" Aaron groused.

Darius nodded, moving away from her bedside to help Aaron to his feet. "The poison is gone. You have done the hardest part," he explained. "You have kept watch over her while we were spurred to action. Wait a little longer. She will greet you on the morrow." With a nod to Tiffin, the etherae exited the room.

Alone with his family, Tiffin stared at his father. "If Darius says she'll be okay, she'll be okay," Tiffin consoled.

His father stared back, brows furrowing. "How do you have such faith in this person you've met barely two days ago?"

"If you had seen what I had seen, your faith would be greater. And his friends are knights, Dad. They told me that he's so far past a level one hundred class etherae that they can't really measure it. He's the most powerful etherae in the world."

His father was quiet, assessing the information. "Level one hundred is the highest?"

Tiffin shrugged. "Sort of. Most people never reach that level, but it's not unheard of. I don't think they know how to measure anything higher."

Tiffin watched the words land on his father before he continued. "Actually, Darius thinks I have some natural skills with animals. That is why the goats respond to me. Why I can ride Gertrude so well. Dad, I think I talked to the dragon."

His father's eyebrows met his hairline, neck stiff and slightly backwards, lips twisted into a sort of grimace. "Maybe you'd better tell me what happened."

Tiffin sat on one side of his aunt, while his father sat in the chair at her bedside. He recounted his adventure again from the time he left the castle to the time he returned, but this time, he highlighted all the times he'd had encounters with animals. As he did so, he realized that in context of his natural powers, the whole story changed.

Of course, the wolf had followed and protected him. It

hadn't been the smell of food. It was something about Tiffin himself that had called out to the creature without knowing he'd done it. Of course, Gertrude rode faster and harder than she ever had without complaint. Of course, the stiguine had allowed him to remove its restraints. And the dreams he'd had about being eaten by the dragon and then soaring in flight with it supported the theory. He wasn't dreaming—he was living their connection.

"Dad," Tiffin implored, "Darius says I have a gift. And...that he would mentor me."

Aaron sighed. "We've talked about this, Tiffin. I need you at the smithy. And we don't have the coin for the supplies you'll need to teach you how to do something you're already doing."

Tiffin wished his father had a wife to make him more reasonable but kept silent on the matter. "I understand. But the training is not forever. I told him about your objections. He says he can arrange for someone to help while I'm training."

Aaron's mouth opened, but a distinctly feminine voice spoke instead.

"It sounds like a marvelous idea."

Tiffin nearly jumped off the bed as his father dropped on his knees beside the bed.

"Helen!" he gasped.

The gentle smile on her face was enough to bring Tiffin instantly to tears.

"Aunt Helen," he welcomed, voice cracking.

Her berry-colored lips quirked up, and she looked like she could fall asleep again at any moment. Her cheeks were pink, and she was no longer sweating.

"My darling nephew," she greeted, hand caressing his cheek. "Where have you been, and why haven't you bathed? You smell atrocious."

Tiffin and his father burst into laughter before his father scooped her into a giant hug and kissed the top of her head.

"I thought we'd lost you, sis," he sobbed.

She hugged him back weakly, chuckling. "Okay, okay. I still have to breathe," she croaked. "I'm too ornery to leave you that easily."

Aaron released her, resting her head on a pillow.

"I don't know what you're so worried about. I've had a little nap, and I feel so much better," Helen excused. "Why are you so upset?"

"Helen, you've been unconscious for more than a week," Tiffin's father exclaimed. "Tiffin made a pilgrimage to the mountains to find a dragon to collect one of its scales to cure you."

Her eyes widened. "You cured me?"

"Well," Tiffin hesitated. "No. Darius did. He's a grand master etherae. We rescued him while we were searching for the dragon that burned all the fields and poisoned you. It was a stiguine."

"Well, that explains the smell at least," she murmured.

"How do you feel?" Aaron questioned.

She frowned. "Like my stomach is trying to kill me. But better." She yawned wide, exposing all of her teeth to them.

"You should sleep," Aaron counseled, patting her shoulder. "I'll go get him washed up. We'll come back with food. And I'll get the etherae to bring you something for the pain if they can."

Aaron guided Tiffin out of the room, closing the door

gently behind them. "You know the kitchen staff. Can you round up something for her? I'll find the etherae."

Tiffin nodded and hurried off, winding his way through the castle to the kitchen. Myra was there, and she reached for him as he passed through the door.

"I hear you're quite the hero," she greeted, tucking him against herself and scuffing his hair. "You could use a good washing though."

He laughed. "That's what Aunt Helen said."

"Said?" she repeated, frozen still.

He nodded. "She's awake, and we think she might be hungry."

"Oh, praise be!" She threw her hands in the air, then barked at half the others working nearby. Her voice cracked when she spoke to him again. "We'll bring up dinner. Your father still there?"

Tiffin nodded.

"I've never seen a more devoted brother," she mused. "I think half my kitchen has taken a shine to him. Big, strong man, he is."

Tiffin drew back. "Yeah...I'm going to get cleaned up now."

"And where exactly do you think you'll do that?" Myra scolded. "Come on with ya. I've got a place." She led him from the kitchen, sneaking down a pathway he was unfamiliar with. She looked around, and seeing they were alone, pulled up a tapestry, and pushed in behind it, dragging him with her.

Chapter 11

Before Tiffin could work out what was going on, Myra closed a door behind them. They were in a dark, narrow passageway. She pressed him forward.

"This is where the etherae prepare for ceremonies. There is a natural spring in this room. We're not allowed to use it, but we're expected to clean it up," she grumbled. "I think for our town hero, we can make an exception."

Tiffin could hear the running water as soon as she mentioned it. The hallway opened up into a surprisingly well-lit space. In the floor was a sunken space full of water that bubbled up from the center. It followed a pathway to the edge of the wall and disappeared. A series of tiny windows highlighted the smooth walls with streaming blocks of daylight.

Myra bustled about the room, opening cabinets and pulling free towels. She laid out a small cloth, a scrub brush, and a jar next to the tub.

"When you're finished, dry up with one of these towels. I'll see if I can't find something for you to put on," she offered. "You can't wear those again till they've been washed.

I'll leave it for you in the hallway here." She pointed just beyond the doorway. "Be quick."

Like a whirlwind, she was gone.

Tiffin looked around uncomfortably. What if someone else came in? The last thing he wanted was to get caught in the bath by someone, let alone an etherae in a private space. He wasted no time stripping off his dirty clothes and piling them at the doorway. The pile on the floor was green and muddy, and he cringed thinking he had touched his aunt with the offending items.

He dipped one toe hesitantly into the bathwater, expecting to flinch at the cold. However, the water was almost warm. No longer concerned about the temperature, Tiffin submerged himself up to his neck. It was the most wonderful experience he'd ever had bathing. If it was like this all the time, he'd do it more often. Maybe being an etherae came with more perks than just powers.

Once he'd given himself time to adjust to the luxurious comfort, Tiffin inspected the items Myra had laid out for him. He opened the jar, sniffing its contents timidly. It smelled like the evergreen trees on the mountains and spices he didn't recognize.

He scooped some on the cloth and began working it over his body. He couldn't believe how quickly his hands cleaned up or how much dirt he found in places he thought were clean. He scrubbed himself from top to bottom, eyes wide as the dirty water flowed naturally away. He reached for the brush, scrubbing his hair, fingernails, toes, and any other stubborn spots.

By the time he finished, he barely recognized himself. Tiffin wrapped a dark blue towel around himself, marveling at the water beading on his shoulders. He had even used the jar's contents over his hair, combing it with his fingers away from his eyes so he could see. Wet tendrils of hair clumped on his forehead, and he slicked them back.

Warily, he peeked around the corner into the hallway. His clothing was gone, and he wondered briefly if it had gotten up and walked away. There was a neat stack of fresh clothing in its place. Tiffin squeezed into the trousers. The loose shirt fell over his head easily, and he topped it off with the remaining vest and belt. A fresh pair of boots sat nearby, and he tugged them onto his feet. His last pair had been tight, but these were larger, and he wiggled his toes happily.

He wished he had a mirror. These were finer clothes than he had ever worn. Unsure what to do with his damp towel, he rolled it up and set it where his dirty clothes had been.

Remembering Myra's admonition to be quick, he scurried down the hall and listened at the door before letting himself out into the hallway. He sneaked through the corridors until he reached his aunt's room.

A small table covered in meats, and breads, and soups, and cheeses, and sweets was stationed in the corner with two empty plates, and Tiffin's stomach grumbled.

Aaron was at Helen's bedside holding a plate of food. He was feeding her a bite of porridge, and Tiffin rushed to take over.

"Eat, Dad," Tiffin murmured. He lifted the spoon to her lips and held steady till she accepted it.

From the corner of his eye, Tiffin saw his father rise to gather a plate for himself.

"Where's your plate?" Helen asked.

"I'm not hungry," he replied, scooping up another spoonful for her.

"That is a lie," she teased, pinching his thigh. "You were born hungry and haven't stopped eating since we met. Get a plate. I'll enjoy it more if you're eating, too."

He resigned himself to obey and made up a quick plate before resuming his place at her side. He nibbled at the food, staring at her mostly uneaten portion.

"You are so clean. And you smell good," she complimented with a smile, shifting in her seated position on the bed. "Your father tells me you had quite an adventure. Did you really set out all alone?" she questioned. She picked a morsel of bread from the slice and ate it.

He launched into the tale without hesitation, telling her all about the wolf and the knights happening upon his fire. "Wolf got between us and would have torn them up if I asked."

He didn't even hear the door open, but everyone was startled when Darius spoke up. "I witnessed him with the wolf. It was otherworldly."

Tiffin stood, nodding.

Darius waved a hand at him. "Sit. Rest. You have earned it." He turned his attention to address Helen. "Word reached me that you had returned to us already."

Helen shifted again, straightening. "I've always been an over achiever."

Darius drew closer, tilting her chin up for inspection.

Tiffin watched as the etherae scanned her face, touching her ears and hands. He asked her many questions and finally declared her on the mend.

"I am sure that you would much prefer to get to your

own surroundings where there is more peace than in a castle like this. But you have undergone a severe illness. I would feel more at ease if you would rest with us a bit longer till we are sure that you are fully recovered."

Helen's cheeks were flushed, and Tiffin thought she might be short of breath as she answered, "Yes, that sounds very sensible."

Tiffin squeezed her hand. "Yes, Aunt Helen. You need to be healthy."

The door burst open, banging against the walls.

"HELEN!" The princess barreled through the room, jumping on the bed, scattering all the plates, and hugging Helen around the neck.

As the young girl launched herself at the bed, Aaron, Tiffin, and Darius all jumped, reaching for plates and bowls with varying degrees of success.

Helen wrapped her arms around the girl and embraced her lightly. "I'm glad to see you too, Narette."

"Princess," Darius cautioned. "Your companion is still weak, and we must give her time to heal."

The princess's face was damp as she pulled away, composing herself in a fashion more befitting of her station. She blinked twice, folding her hands in her lap. "I was not certain you would wake. Please, don't ever get sick again," she begged.

Helen mustered a small laugh. "I will endeavor to be more careful in the future," she promised. "You all are really making quite a fuss over this."

"No," the princess refuted. "You were unconscious for more than a week."

"And you breathed fire," Tiffin added.

Helen and the princess turned their eyes on him, mouths hanging open.

"You did," Tiffin assured. "It was blue. And then you were encased in purple fire all over."

Helen lifted her hands, inspecting her skin and rubbing at her wrists. She looked to the etherae for answers.

"Yes," Darius explained. "The poison began inside your belly. The cure ignites the poison, burning itself out as it permeates your skin. Only the poison is burned."

Helen shook her head. "You are a miracle worker."

Darius met her face boldly. "No. An etherae. It is your nephew who saved the day with the dragon. Even I would not have had his success so easily."

"Speaking of," Aaron interjected. "Would it be possible to have what's left of the scale to keep at the house?"

Darius looked between father and son. "Yes, I think that would be a fitting trophy. I extracted the marrow of the first scale to save your lovely sister. I will bring the husk to you, and once I have harvested the second, you are welcome to it as well."

Aaron backed a few steps away from the princess. "Sis, I see you are in good hands here. I think perhaps Tiffin should rest at home."

"At this hour?" the princess exclaimed. "Never. We will find a place for you. You can go home after breakfast." She launched to her delicate feet and marched out the door, barking orders at the person nearest.

Helen chuckled. "It's good to be the princess," she muttered. She took her brother's hand. "I love you. Thank you for your kind ministrations all this while."

"It was the least I could do for my favorite sister," he

replied.

"You have no other sisters," she sassed.

He shrugged. "Still my favorite." He kissed the top of her head. "Rest well."

Helen opened her arms to Tiffin. "I want a hug from you, you brilliant man." She squeezed him carefully, then eased herself back down onto the bed.

"I will check on you as well tomorrow," Darius promised, then with a small wave moved himself into the hallway.

Tiffin followed after him, rushing to catch up. "Thank you," he murmured.

"You're welcome," Darius replied, and Tiffin noticed he was bracing his elbow against the wall.

"I'm sorry. Please. Go rest. I don't know how you have the strength to walk after what you've been through." Tiffin stepped out of his way.

"I have survived worse," he replied. "I will see you tomorrow, and hopefully our friends will join us."

True to her word, the princess had quarters arranged near Aunt Helen, and Tiffin and his father bedded down. Tiffin didn't remember his head hitting the pillow. He had not anticipated the way his back and legs would ache when he rolled over the following day. He remembered the stretches Pierce had shown him and as soon as he was able to roll out of bed, he maneuvered himself into them. Pain seared through his body, but he sucked it back until it eased.

He realized with a start that he was alone in the room. Before he could panic, the door opened, and his father entered. "Oh, good. You're awake. I've never seen you sleep this late before."

Tiffin frowned. "How's Aunt Helen?"

"Good. Asking for you. You should get dressed and join her. The kitchen brought a bunch of food for us in her room."

Tiffin nodded, reaching for his breeches and preparing himself to be seen.

His father cleared his throat softly. "The princess is in there as well. She has a lot to say."

Tiffin froze with one arm in his shirt, the rest stalled awkwardly over his head. "Oh."

"As a goat farmer, you have no hope of having a conversation with her ilk," his father pointed out.

"I know," Tiffin agreed, pulling on the rest of his clothes. "I'm always careful not to address her directly unless I have to."

"Smart," his father approved. "But perhaps...a fully trained etherae may have more access to her friendship."

Tiffin could tell his father was hinting at something, but he was too afraid to ask for fear of being wrong. "What?" he finally blurted.

"Master Darius has seen your aunt this morning and brought me the first scale. We have been discussing your training," his father clarified.

Tiffin stared in shock. "My *training*?" he repeated.

His father nodded. "I know it's something you've always wanted. And while we have many responsibilities, this illness with your aunt reminded me that we also have responsibilities to the kingdom. If it had not been for your willingness to do what needed to be done, and the etherae and his knight friends, we would have lost your aunt. They had no obligation to us other than their oath to protect the kingdom.

And it will be a struggle, but Master Darius and I agree that it would be a crime not to capitalize on this gift you have."

Tears blurred Tiffin's vision, and he threw his arms around his father. "Thank you," he whispered.

Aaron squeezed him back tightly enough for his bones to pop. "I am so proud of the man you are becoming."

With the promise of education ahead of him and his aunt on the mend, Tiffin realized suddenly. "What happened to the goats?"

"I sent word to Gimble. He's been looking after them, but he does not have your gift for the small creatures. He's invented some very creative exclamations," he said with a chuckle.

Tiffin clapped his hands over his face. "I didn't even think about them when we left, Dad. Some animal expert I am."

Aaron patted his shoulder. "This is part of the man you will become. Experience will teach you to think ahead. You have shouldered more burden at your age than you should have."

He shrugged. "We do what we need to," Tiffin replied. "Just like you've always said."

Tiffin was grateful to discover that the knights had also returned from their quest, and after they had been fed, cleaned and properly dressed, he made introductions to his aunt. They made fast friends, and Darius finally released his aunt to return home two days later.

Tiffin and his father gathered their few supplies, including both hollowed scales, into a wagon on loan from the castle. Gertrude had no protestation when hitched to the wagon, and Tiffin expected it was due to the horse at her side.

He recognized the sleek black male they'd taken from the bandits who had tried to rob them. He smirked, patting her side and promising to be right back.

Aaron had gone ahead to collect his sister, and Tiffin scurried to catch up. He felt the now-familiar bite of the princess's dagger in his boot and sighed with relief when she was with his aunt. His father whisked Helen into his arms to carry, and she slapped lightly at his shoulders to be set down.

It was the perfect distraction. Tiffin stood close to the princess and passed the cloth-wrapped dagger to her discreetly. "Thank you for the loan. It came in handy."

The princess's cheek dimpled as she accepted it, quickly tucking it inside her sleeve. "I am glad for any aid I was able to provide."

Tiffin nodded, looking to his aunt for assistance.

The princess did the same, then she hugged Aunt Helen. "Please rest for a few days. I will manage without my braids until you are well. I have been studying my philosophy and my history, though they are dull."

Helen arched a brow at her. "Many would give their pinky finger to have your dull studies."

The princess sighed. "And I have nearly completed my needlepoint. I will let you be the judge of my progress."

Helen took Tiffin's arm. "I'm certain you have made great strides. You always do when you focus," she complimented. "I will see you soon."

"But not too soon."

Helen nodded, nudging Tiffin toward the door.

Chapter 12

Smoke billowed from the smithy, but not through the chimney. Aaron yelled again, this time throwing the cloth over his shoulder out into the yard where the goats were hopping about and bleating.

Tiffin was distracted from where he and Darius were stationed at the edge of the forest honing his innate skill with animals. His father had been trying for hours to re-light the forge, and Tiffin wondered what the problem was. From the moment Darius had placed the two dragon scales in his hands, he had been like a man possessed, and he had rushed to the shop to see what would happen when heated. They had been away for so long with Aunt Helen that the usually blistering fire was ice cold. Tiffin couldn't remember ever seeing the smithy dead like this.

"You will never pass your levels if you don't focus," Darius corrected from his position atop a large boulder.

He wanted to groan. He'd liked Darius much better when he was chained inside the stinky house during their quest. That was uncharitable, and he regretted the thought instantly.

A kreakcoon was munching on a nearby patch of onion grass. The entire area smelled strongly of the plant, and between that and his family, he couldn't rein in his attention.

"Touch the ground," Darius instructed. "Feel the vibration of the earth beneath his feet. Sense his breathing. His heartbeat. Touch the fire within him."

The directions were clear enough except they meant nothing. What did he mean by touching the fire within the creature with his hand on the ground?

He knelt, splaying his fingers against the damp earth. Sharp mineral smells pricked his senses, the soil soft at the surface. He dug his fingers in till it compacted and closed his eyes. His breathing slowed, and the green plants and onion grass overwhelmed the minerals. He heard grass being ripped up by the roots. It reminded him of Gertrude having her fill in a plentiful field.

The kreakcoon was completely unbothered by Tiffin. It ate without so much as casting a glance in his direction. Its long claws buried themselves into the earth beneath its feet, loosening the roots of the plants it planned to devour next. He anticipated its movement as it started to back up to pull up another patch of tender blades.

Tiffin imagined his full belly when he ate the sweets from the castle. Content. Peaceful. Warm.

Tiffin's belly felt hot as though he was eating the onion grass. He opened his eyes, and the beast was less than a foot away, its tail nearly brushing his ankle.

Without a second thought, Tiffin launched himself onto the creature's back.

Its dark blue hide glimmered as the dragon jerked to life, trying to unseat him. Immediately, Tiffin slid to the ground, and the creature scampered away, turning on him and growling.

Darius intervened, jumping between them and tapping the ground with his staff. He looked at Tiffin. "You thought jump scaring an animal that can breathe molten fire was your best first move?"

Tiffin grumbled. "It was right there," he complained.

Pinching the bridge of his nose, Darius stood still for a moment without a word.

This was not a good sign. They'd barely been training, but this expression usually meant the lesson was about to end.

"I'll do better," Tiffin promised. "Maybe I could...offer it a snack."

"That would be a better start."

The animal had moved on to rooting around near the base of a tree a few feet away. It clawed and snarled at the bits of bark it tossed aside.

Tiffin noted how the thick roots were no match for the beast's sheer power. They shredded like parchment and were pushed away just as easily.

"When you first met Gertrude, how did you approach her?" Darius pressed.

He thought about it for a while. "I wanted her to know I wasn't a threat. I brought her an apple."

"The kreakcoon is much the same; smaller even," he encouraged. "What do you think it's searching for?"

"Truffles. Like a pig," Tiffin guessed.

Darius nodded his head in approval. "Very good."

Tiffin gathered a bundle of onion grass, doing his best to keep the scowl from his face. The pungent smell made his nose twitch, and he suspected he'd be smelling it on his hands all night. He inched closer, speaking softly.

The animal stopped digging, and its nose began scenting the air. It pinpointed Tiffin quickly, and he froze.

After a short consideration, the beast shook its claws free of the detritus of the tree and stared Tiffin down.

He bowed his head reverently, keeping both hands in sight the same way as he had with the stiguine. Then he crouched low, holding the peace offering out for the taking.

The kreakcoon clucked its tongue, and Tiffin thought its teeth chattered. He kept his eyes focused on the ground until footsteps sounded. Tiffin placed his free hand on the ground, feeling the creature's weight as it lumbered toward him.

He looked up when he saw its feet come to a stop a foot away. Its long snout snuffled at the ends of the grass in his hand. It was afraid.

Tiffin placed the grass on the ground between them, daring to study the animal openly. Its eyelids closed for several counts before it snapped up the treat, a dry black tongue darting out to touch the blades.

It took more cajoling, and Tiffin's palms were turning green as he fed the animal for another few minutes. It rested on its belly inches from him, closing its eyes.

"Is it asleep?" he asked.

"I don't believe so," Darius answered. "You're earning its trust. What would you do next with a horse?"

The process was slow, but Tiffin worked through it, first letting the kreakcoon adjust to his touch before he stood next to it. He stroked its back slowly until he felt its weight shift and press into his hand.

He paused at its mid-back, and the burbling in its belly

shivered under his fingertips. Screwing up his courage, Tiffin placed both hands on its side and gently lifted one leg to straddle it.

The kreakcoon's body tensed as Tiffin rested his weight on its back. He remained still, palms on its shoulder blades.

Darius beamed at him.

His patience was rewarded when the creature shambled forward with Tiffin still on its back. He thanked the creature, petting its neck and urging it to speed up.

His legs relaxed around its body, and before he realized what was happening, it had picked up speed and they were headed toward the gentle hill leading to the forge. It roared, and Tiffin yelled along with it as they galloped ahead.

Tiffin held onto the back of the kreakcoon for dear life. Its rough hide was slippery against his breeches, and each bounce from its four legs windmilling over the terrain made his backside pucker. The creature was roughly three feet off the ground, much shorter than any horse he had ridden, and he struggled to keep his feet from catching on the dirt path below them.

Seeing his father and aunt ahead of him, he yelled for the beast to stop. It took three tries before it listened, so gleeful was it in its all-out sprint. Its long, flat face wriggled ahead of him, spewing droplets of saliva that nearly landed on his family.

Darius was behind him on a horse, slowing down. "Very good," he complimented. "Now see if you can light the forge."

Tiffin looked back at him. It was a brilliant idea, and he wished he'd thought of it.

The kreakcoon was panting beneath him, wriggling left

and right. It wanted direction. Tiffin reached for the fire inside the dragon's belly. He could feel it swirling somewhere between his thighs, the grass and truffles and tree roots all roiling hotly. He urged it forward, maneuvering it through the door which was barely wider than the creature.

His father and aunt jumped aside, their faces openly displaying their shock.

"Tiffin, what are you doing?" his father yelled, running after him.

"I'm lighting the forge, Dad. Like Master Darius told me."

"He said *if!*" his father enunciated. "This is our life, Tiffin."

"Dad," he persisted. "I've got this."

Tiffin compelled the kreakcoon as close to the mouth of the pit as he dared, then laid a hand on the back of its neck until the flames gurgled. Its long jaw cracked open a finger's width, revealing two rows of teeth. A ripple at the back of its throat pulsed under his palm before a narrow blue flame poured from the creature, splattering the innards of the forge.

Immediately the flames turned white, exploding in fire.

When Tiffin could see the forge was fully ablaze, he removed his hand from the back of the kreakcoon's neck, and the outpouring stopped.

Aaron stared in disbelief.

Darius's face quirked in a self-satisfied smirk. "I hope our training isn't interfering with your real work," he murmured.

Helen stifled a giggle, and her cheeks turned pink. Tiffin thought she sounded like the princess in that moment—much younger than her years.

"I think that's enough dragon lessons for one day," Darius announced. "Those goats of yours need attention."

"You're not leaving, are you?" Helen asked.

"I really should. I have intruded on your merry household long enough," Darius replied, slowly turning his horse one degree at a time.

"Nonsense," she insisted. "I've extra provisions sent from the castle in thanks for Tiffin's quest. You should join us. In case..." She trailed off briefly. "Well, I have been feeling a bit tired of late."

"Ah yes. The lingering effects of nearly dying from dragon poison." Darius nodded knowingly, then sighed, inching his mare toward the hitching post usually reserved for customers. "As a servant of the kingdom, I couldn't very well leave one of it is residents alone if they are unwell."

Helen pivoted on her toe and marched into the house.

Darius slipped from his mount, snapped his fingers, and pointed to the post. The reins knotted themselves around it instantly, and the etherae disappeared behind Aunt Helen before the door shut.

Tiffin looked at his father. "What was that?"

Aaron shook his head. "Son, I'm not sure you're old enough for that conversation yet."

Understanding dawned, and Tiffin stiffened as he dismounted and released his dragon with a stroke of gratitude over one of its ears. The creature reared its hind legs, then scampered back to the forest.

"Darius has never mentioned it to me," Tiffin grumbled, watching as his father prepared his tools to begin a new piece.

"As well he shouldn't." Aaron lifted the smaller of the two hollow dragon scales into his largest crucible and eased it into the forge.

Tiffin watched in awe as at first, nothing happened despite the incinerating temperatures. And then the milky green scale began glowing, and the flames turned green as they licked over the interior surfaces.

His father's cheeks rounded as his lips curved upwards in delight. "Oh, this is going to be fun," he mumbled.

Tiffin watched for a while with his father, but then he left and tended the goats before he eased to the door of the house. He pressed his ear to it, relieved to hear sounds of voices inside and the unmistakable creaking of the rocking chair railings rolling back and forth.

He eased the door open, announcing himself immediately.

"Tiffin, bring me some potatoes from the larder, please," Helen called.

He recognized the sound of his aunt chopping things in the kitchen. He knew when she said larder, she was speaking of a wooden crate they stored under the house. It was cooler there and their vegetables lasted longer than in the heat of the house. But she used the name for it like at the castle—he suspected to impress the etherae who occupied the rocking chair, keeping watch.

He returned with the requested items, depositing them on the table next to her. She smiled sweetly at him, and he swore her cheeks had darkened to red.

"I'm not sure Dad's coming in now that he's got the fires back. You should've seen his face when he put the scale in."

Darius sparked at the statement. "He put it in the fire? The stiguine is a fire dragon."

Tiffin nodded. "I think that's what gave him the idea. It

burned green when the inside caught," he exuberated.

Darius's mouth made a moue. "Interesting. Are you sure your father isn't a fire worker?"

"I somehow doubt it if he couldn't start his own forge," his aunt replied with a wry chuckle.

Tiffin laughed.

"With no training, even the most amazing talent might not know they could say, communicate with dragons," Darius leveled.

The laughter died on Tiffin's lips, and he bit his lower lip. "You're right."

"You did well today, young man," Darius complimented. "You've improved greatly since we began your training."

Tiffin straightened up and offered a tiny bow. "I know I still have a long way to go."

"Did you feed the goats?" Aunt Helen asked.

"Yes," he replied. He glanced at his aunt's tight jaw and wondered what she was upset about. He turned to Darius. "Whatever happened to the amulet we found around the dragon's neck?"

The etherae shifted in the rocker. "I've been working on it," he replied. "It is definitely infused with power. I think I can use it to trace back to Rufus and find out where he is hiding. He's not going to be happy knowing that he's lost his dragon."

"Are we safe?" Tiffin questioned quietly.

Darius didn't answer at first, and when he did, his words were slow and deliberate. "I believe that until Rufus has been stopped, no one is safe, regardless of their role in taking away his weapon."

"What can I do to help?"

"Keep training. The more you know to protect yourself and those around you, the more aid you are to us all. When you feed the goats, communicate with them. When you ride Gertrude, sense her. Unless you are asleep, work. Train your own mind. I will guide you during our lessons."

Tiffin should have expected the answer. Work, work, work was the answer to everything. Still, he craved knowledge, and he probed his instructor further, scraping one fingernail against the tabletop. "I don't understand what he expects to gain?"

"I am still trying to work that out," Darius confessed.

"Pierce said you trained together. Did you know him well?"

Darius nodded, pinching his lips between his thumb and forefinger. "We were rivals during our training. Always vying for the top spot. I always thought it was a little fun. Motivation to keep each other sharp."

"It sounds like it was more than that to him," Aunt Helen added.

Darius nodded. "There is a stigma among the etherae that those who are born gifted are...better than those who are not. There are strengths and weaknesses on both sides."

"People will always find ways to hold one another down," Helen consoled.

"When the plague passed through fifteen years ago, we thought it took him with it," Darius finished.

Helen winced, glancing at Tiffin. "I remember it well. I moved in with Aaron and Tiffin after it passed." She dropped the peeled and diced potatoes into the stew pot and pressed the iron rod into the fireplace. "What made you think he'd died in the plague?"

Darius shrugged. "We received word from a trusted advisor. Pierce had seen him during his illness. Said he was near death at the time. When we received word that he had passed, we had no reason to doubt it."

Helen cleaned her knife and wiped down the counters. She took a seat at the table. "So how do you know this is him if you were so certain he was dead?"

"He hired the miscreants who abducted me," Darius replied. "They thought I would be an easy target because I don't look like a knight. But I've learned to put up a rather good fight in my lifetime. When they finally overcame me, I awoke in a hovel. He chained me there, tortured me for days, then left me for dead for a fortnight before Tiffin and the knights discovered me."

"All the more reason to stay and preserve your strength," Helen cautioned. "The body does not recover quickly after such malnourishment."

"Your thoughtful care is well received." Darius smiled.

Tiffin's stomach grumbled at the sight. He had grown accustomed to the etherae's presence over the past week. Darius was friendly, but he was also demanding. Tiffin swore that nothing he ever did was right but for rare moments when he overheard the mentor talking about it to others. To see his eyes narrowing as he looked at Helen...there was something not sinister but almost predatory. He didn't like it. As his pupil, though, Tiffin stilled his tongue.

His best bet was to change the subject. "How does the amulet work?" Tiffin quizzed. "Was it a form of mind control?"

"Yes, exactly that," Darius replied. "The amulet must contact flesh to function. That is why it was so tightly bound around the dragon's neck."

"And why you wrapped it in a cloth once it was free," Tiffin guessed.

"No. I covered it because it acts as an eye, showing Rufus everything the dragon can see. Covering it blinds him. I am trying to determine the specific working used for the binding. If I can follow the bond, I should at least know where he is hiding."

"What does he hope to gain by burning down the entire kingdom?" Helen mused.

"Power," Darius answered. "Although what he plans to do with it, I can't be sure."

"If he went through the trouble to abduct you and leave you for dead, I think he has a score to settle with you. And he knows where you are," Helen warned.

Darius nodded. "I hope I have what it takes to withstand him."

Helen sighed. "Is there anything we can do to help?" she asked.

He shrugged. "I'm working on it. But I don't want you anywhere near the action," he insisted.

"I am no weakling," she countered. "I can help."

Darius leaned forward in the rocker, placing his hand over hers. "If there is a task for which no one else would be better suited than you, I will set you to it," he promised.

Tiffin turned a little green. "I'm going to watch Dad work with the scale. I'll be back for dinner."

"Clean up while you're out there," his aunt called.

Chapter 13

Tiffin gave one more proud spin for Darius, who clapped. When he stopped, the etherae scooted closer, touching the smooth surface of the translucent green breast plate Tiffin sported.

Darius circled him several times, admiring the fittings that held it together.

"Dad says that it didn't melt like iron, even in the dragon flames, but it became..." Tiffin searched for the right word.

"Malleable," Darius supplied. He studied the work at a distance. "It appears to be impenetrable."

Tiffin shrugged. "I'd hardly say we've tried it out. Dad said once it had cooled, he hit it with his hammer as hard as he could, and not even a scratch."

"Yet it appears as glass. One could assume it would be equally fragile," the etherae rationalized.

Tiffin knocked his knuckles against his chest, and a *thunk* reverberated around Darius's chambers.

"What do you say we test it out today?" Darius suggested.

A grin answered him. "I've been dying for you to say that," Tiffin replied. He recommended multiple courtyards to begin their training and raced for the door, leaving Darius in his proverbial dust.

"Those are all near the princess's private gardens," Darius pointed out. "Should our tests prove your armor penetrable...are you sure you want her to see your guts?"

Tiffin didn't answer. He hadn't thought he would be that easy to read, but he supposed the man didn't get to be a grand master without some modicum of wisdom.

"Be careful giving out your heart," Darius cautioned.

The irony of the statement did not surpass him.

A slow clapping noise startled them both. "Sage advice, indeed," a deep voice called as its owner applauded.

Darius and Tiffin turned toward the sound. Tiffin didn't recognize the newcomer, and he glanced at his mentor for guidance.

The etherae's jaw was clenched, eyes narrowed to angry slits. Darius lifted both hands. Tiffin recognized the offensive stance and prepared himself to crouch.

"Rufus," Darius grumbled.

Tiffin was grateful for the armor he had been showing off moments ago. He rested his right hand on the hilt of his sword.

The other man looked entirely harmless upon first glance. He was roughly the same height as Darius, but thicker. His hair was like the inside of a sapling, pale and blond, hanging in wispy strands around his shoulders. A grotesque scar stretched from one eyebrow down to his jaw, gray from age. There was nothing else exceptional about his features save the self-satisfied grin that bared his teeth.

"Darius," he murmured.

Tiffin's pulse raced, body tensing and knees bending.

His aunt was in the castle. The princess was in the castle. He scooted one foot toward the door.

"Your young apprentice is more foolish than he looks if he doesn't think I see him attempting to escape," Rufus said. He turned his hazel eye on Tiffin. "What in the world is that made from anyway? Glass?" He laughed. "It's like doing the work for me."

"He is no concern of yours," Darius growled, stepping between Tiffin and Rufus. "What are you trying to accomplish? First, you take control of a dragon, then you burn down all the food sources, then you poison the people. There will be no one left to control."

Rufus laughed. "Is that what you think this is?"

"We thought you died in the plague," Darius reproached.

He shrugged. "I wanted you to. You were holding me back."

"You made it especially easy," Darius taunted.

Tiffin listened to the exchange and realized this was his chance. He focused on making his footfalls silent. Instead of aiming for the door, he eased backwards. At any moment, Rufus could turn and face him, but he was taking the bait.

Rufus's voice was slow and melodic as though he had all the time in the world. As though he'd been planning this confrontation for a lifetime. He chuckled, folding his hands in front of himself. "Of course, I couldn't compete with you, power-born as you are."

Even amidst his escape plan, the words were hurtful. Tiffin was power-born too. The words sounded vulgar in the voice of his mentor's rival. He reached for the tapestry portraying a library.

"You can't compete with me," Darius agreed. "You can study and train and know all the right methods. But you will never have my well of power."

Tiffin's fingers froze on the fabric, and he looked back at Darius. He had never heard such words come out of the man before, never referenced the vastness of his own power. He heard many others do it, but Darius had never claimed greatness.

"I knew it!" Rufus cried, hands thrown into the air. He leveled one at Darius, pointing angrily. "There it is. Finally! You've made me wait a great many years to hear you admit it." He sighed, lowering his arms and spinning in delight.

If Tiffin had simply disappeared as he had been planning, Rufus would not have seen him while doing a glory turn, and he would definitely not have stopped in his tracks.

"Where do you think you're going?" Rufus snarled.

Tiffin didn't bother to answer. He slipped behind the tapestry and pushed through the door, slamming it shut behind himself. He had always wondered why a rod was mounted on it with a matching slot in the stone wall, but as he slid the locking bar into place, he understood.

He heard Rufus slam against the other side of the door before Tiffin bolted down the hallway. What sounded like an explosion burst behind him, but he didn't stop.

He ran until he reached a door and exited the corridor, not worried if anyone saw him. "PIERCE!" he yelled.

Several servants stopped in their tracks, and a guard was clanking toward him. "Young man!" he yelled.

"Get Pierce!" Tiffin cried. "Master Darius is under attack!"

Tiffin kept running. He called for Pierce and Elias and

even Kaiden as he ran, but all he got was yelled at for the ruckus. He skidded around the corner to Princess Narette's chambers, barely remaining upright. He saw the guards outside her door and detoured rather than raise their hackles. He made straight for the courtyard she liked best. Surely his aunt would be there.

He was running out of breath as he burst into the garden.

A pair of guards tripped him as he raced by, and Tiffin landed face first in a patch of grass less than ten yards away from his aunt and her charge. Tiffin struggled upright and launched himself toward them again, and he could hear the guards chasing after him.

Aunt Helen turned to see the source of the noise, and when her eyes fell on Tiffin, she jumped up from the blanket where she and the princess had been reclining with their morning sweets. "Tiffin!" she yelped.

Tiffin was closing the gap as quickly as his legs would carry him until a sudden weight landed on his back, throwing him roughly to the ground.

"I said stop!" the guard behind him yelled against his ear.

Tiffin grumbled beneath the weight of the larger man until it was suddenly gone, and he thought his arm might be yanked out of place by the guards wrenching him to his feet.

"What are you doing?" Helen demanded, stalking toward him.

"It's Rufus! He's here," Tiffin gasped even as he was being yanked backwards. He strained against their tight hold, bowing toward his aunt.

"In the castle?" she worried, glancing around at their surroundings. She lifted her gaze skyward, and Tiffin noticed suddenly that the clouds were speeding by them, the blue of the sky dimming.

"Yes. Darius was holding him off while I escaped to find you."

"Lies," the guard on his right scolded. He drew back his hand to punish Tiffin with a slap to the face, but Helen blocked the blow as she grabbed the man's wrist.

"If he says Rufus is here, then he is, indeed, here."

"He can't go barging into the princess's courtyard," the guard grumbled, yanking at his arm.

"Harold, stop. You know this is my nephew," she said. "And look up, you dolt. The sun doesn't go dark without a storm."

The guard sighed, and Tiffin shrugged out of his grasp. "We have to get you both to safety."

The princess was jogging toward them now. "What is this about?" she questioned.

Helen laid a hand on her shoulder, drawing the girl to her side. "There is a great danger in the castle," she explained.

As the gentle words left her mouth, the winds picked up, sending bits of debris rocketing around them.

"We should go," Helen urged.

The hairs on Tiffin's arms twitched, and he drew his sword, looking around. The earth shook beneath his feet as an explosion reverberated behind him.

He turned to see a plume of debris where a castle spire had once been, and he saw Rufus flying overhead. He tracked the man as he sailed through the air and pressed one hand behind himself toward the door. "Go!"

Thunder rolled as the skies turned an unnatural inky black. Without stars and the moon to light their path, chaos erupted. Guards sprang into motion from their stations across the city, yelling and pulling everyone inside.

Tiffin stumbled backwards as the others started to sprint for the door. The air itched inside his nose, and he searched above him for its origin. A streak of light hurtled toward them. He wouldn't make it to them before it struck, and he leaped for the princess and his aunt in a last-ditch effort to protect them. A bolt of lightning burned the air around them.

Suddenly, his whole world was hot white light as the blast launched him backwards. A high-pitched whistling filled his ears, and bits of wet debris rained down as he rolled to a seated position. Something smelled like burned hair and charred meat.

His vision blurred, and he saw the guard that had been wrenching his arm on the ground, skin black and smoking through the armholes of his breast plate, motionless.

Tiffin should have been toast—literal toast. He checked his limbs, and found them sluggish but functional, before pushing himself upwards. Rain splattered against his head, sizzling as it touched his armor. He yelled, but he couldn't hear anything beyond an intense ringing that threw off his balance.

He needed to move. He could assess what had happened later. Now, he needed to make sure everyone else from the courtyard had found cover. Tiffin shoved himself to his feet, stumbling toward the safety of the keep.

From the corner of his eye, he saw Darius running across the yard outside the walls in the direction he had seen Rufus flying. Sheets of water soaked him to the bone. Lightning cracked the ground in three places in quick succession, following Darius's path.

Tiffin's lips formed the word "inside!" But he heard nothing against the deluge of weather. He grabbed hold of the princess's shoulders, pulling her upright, then reached for his aunt.

A blue flash exploded from the ground, reaching skyward, and thunder crashed around them. Tiffin looked behind him, seeing Rufus on the castle walls two stories above them and a fair distance away. His unkempt hair swirled around his face, glowing in a ghastly halo against the curves of his face.

The terrain was veritably disintegrating beneath their feet, and both the ladies in his charge tumbled to the ground.

Rufus's laugh pierced through the storm, and Tiffin could barely hear himself think. Pressure crushed his skull, and he fell to his knees.

Between the lightning flashes, he could make out the figure of Darius on the ground halfway between himself and the enemy. The etherae's knees were bent, bracing himself against an onslaught of gravel pouring at him so fast it whistled.

His right hand swirled, and Tiffin could see the air around it crackling with power. His left hand was spread in Rufus's direction as if focusing all the gathered energy. Darius's lips barely parted, and the moment they did, a lance of force split through it, throwing Rufus five feet back to land on his back.

Tiffin saw his opportunity, racing ahead to where his aunt lay, prone, wrapped around the princess. He laid hands on each of them, urging them to their feet and dragging them alongside him.

His new armor pinched at the shoulder where the breast

plate met the shoulder guards, but he simply pulled harder at them. Yards separated them from the cover of the keep on the edge of the courtyard, but to Tiffin, it could have been a hundred miles.

He wrenched the door open and pushed the princess through. He cringed as she stumbled, but he was already reaching for his aunt, grabbing any part of her he could and shoving her inside.

The thunder of armor inside was equally deafening to the battle waging outside. It was a welcome din. All the torches inside had somehow been lit, filling the hall with an orange glow.

He ignored the eerie light rippling through the halls, grabbing the door with both hands to pull it closed. Abruptly, the pressure of the winds dragging the door eased as Pierce on one side and Kaiden on the other gripped the door with him. Tiffin's arms cramped as they wrestled it shut.

Elias nearly knocked them down as he slid the heavy locking board into position, and they all slumped to the floor.

"Are you well, princess?" Pierce gasped, pressing himself to his feet to give her aid.

She held a hand to ward him off and nodded. Her hair had broken free of the usual bun at the nape of her neck. With tendrils of gold clung to her face, her clothing drenched and plastered to her, she appeared fragile.

Her face was set in an angry scowl, fists clenched at her side. "Were it not for Tiffin and Helen, I'd be a black spot on the ground. Who is that?" She pointed in the direction of the fight outside.

His aunt wrung out her gown then reached to pull Narette's hair away from her face and back into place. The princess stared at the knights, clearly awaiting an answer.

Tiffin was mesmerized by the way the firelight played across the wet hollow of her throat. She was gasping for breath, and he wondered briefly if she was about to spew fire.

"Rufus," Pierce answered. "He's Darius's nemesis."

"That's how you know he's important," Elias joked. "You can't be important without a nemesis."

Pierce did not share his humor, casting a silencing glance in the other man's direction.

Tiffin rushed to his aunt's side. "I'm sorry I pushed you."

"You did what you needed to." She pressed a hand to his chest. "It seems your dragon's gift has saved me twice. I felt the lightning hit you."

Tiffin looked down at the chest plate his father had fashioned from the dragon's scale. He had felt it too. The lightning bolt had struck dead center, and while he had been knocked off his feet, and possibly unconscious for a moment, the milky green material didn't even show a point of impact. It was as shiny and clean as before the strike.

"Wait till we tell Dad. He won't believe me."

"You're indebted to that dragon," Helen cautioned.

"We're friends, Aunt Helen. He *gave* me the scales."

"You'll be cleaning out his cavern for months to make armor of his old scales," Elias pointed out. "And I'm first."

"Later!" the princess reprimanded. "Now we have to help the master."

"What good can we do out there against those powers?" Pierce balked. "Darius is more than capable."

"You would do well to call him master," his aunt scolded. "And he may be able to take care of himself, but there's a whole village of people in the pathway of their destruction."

Pierce's eyes widened, and his jaw grew slack. "Yes! We have bystanders to save," he announced, leading the charge.

Tiffin followed behind, surprised to see the two women joining them. "Princess, you cannot risk yourself."

She glanced at him as they ran behind the knights. "I may not have the skills you do, but I have my part to play." At that, she broke away from the group and moved down a different corridor.

Helen nearly knocked him down in her haste to keep up. "Be careful, Tiff!" she yelled.

Tiffin wanted to stay with her. His father would kill him if she didn't survive after all they had been through. But the knights were putting distance between him and them, and he scurried to catch up.

This was what being a man meant—trusting loved ones to take care of themselves to protect the kingdom from burning. It meant putting actions to words and not letting fear hold him back. He had skills now, and he was ready to flex.

Tiffin swallowed back his worries and ran.

"The safest place is in the catacombs beneath the keep," Elias indicated.

Pierce nodded his agreement. "Kaiden, take the west side. Elias, take the north. I'll cover the south. Tiffin, go with Elias."

"I want to help Master Darius," Tiffin complained.

"And you will by clearing a path, do you understand?" Pierce retorted.

As they emerged from the castle gates onto the battlefield, Tiffin noted that fires had broken out in half a dozen buildings. Thatch roofs were ablaze, loose embers floating around them. The rain had stopped, but the winds were doing no favors, and Tiffin watched an adjacent building begin to burn.

There was so much noise! People screaming, some throwing buckets of water near the flames. He had no idea where to begin.

"Tiffin! This way!" Elias called.

He followed, breaking off from the others, and he acted without thinking, pulling ladies and children away from the fires and directing them to the safe spaces.

The battle raged between Darius and Rufus, more stone powder filling the air as a variety of surfaces smashed.

Tiffin ran to Elias's side, grabbing him by the arm. "He needs our help," he begged, pointing to the fireball racing across the sky.

Elias sighed. "I know. This first, and then we will help," Elias promised. They ushered the last of the people outside toward the keep. Elias rounded up a few guards to go door to door to free livestock and gather stragglers.

Then the pair ran in the direction of the fight, tagging Pierce and Kaiden to join them. They huddled themselves under the cover of a cart of potatoes that was being delivered when the battle had begun. The air smelled like fresh dirt and starch.

Darius's face was streaked with sweat and concentration, fingers contorted into painful positions.

The winds between his hands twisted into a swirl, and he pushed it toward Rufus with all his force.

Elias leaned in. "If we can attack him from behind, maybe we can stop him long enough for Darius to finish him off."

"I like it," Pierce agreed. "Tell us what to do."

Chapter 14

Hands trembling, Tiffin pulled the saddle tight around the horse's belly. He was the biggest one in the stable, black and strong. He wasn't sure about Elias's plan, but he had no other choice. The giant stallion was calm, nuzzling into his hand when he finished.

"Thank you," he whispered.

He mounted the horse, reaching out with his senses to see what other animals were nearby. The wolf that had accompanied him on his journey was close, and Tiffin called to it.

He sped toward the rendezvous point Elias had set, bouncing along the terrain. He wasn't sure about this plan. Elias was counting on the four of them to sneak up from behind and knock him out. They would be relying on Tiffin to rally any critters nearby to jump into the attack from above and below the ground.

He closed his eyes, letting the horse guide them. The winds howled past his ears. Lightning cracked once overhead, and he looked skyward in time to see the hint of an outline behind the clouds.

Could it be? He stared back as the horse thundered forward, and lightning flashed again. This time, he saw the large figure clearly. It was the stiguine. He was sure of it. He touched one hand to the armor on his chest, and the connection strengthened.

The dragon's unmistakable howl sounded overhead, and Tiffin leaned into the horse's gallop.

"Sorry, Elias," he mumbled to himself. "New plan."

He focused on the top of the place where he had last seen the rival etherae on the castle walls. His silhouette cackled in the darkness. Blasts of power were crackling from his fingertips as he lobbed them at Darius, faster and faster.

His mentor deflected them one after the other, but his steps slowed, and Tiffin watched in horror as he sank to his knees, a dome of invisible power shielding him from both attack and rain. While protected, he was unable to render his own attacks.

Tiffin looked up as the great emerald head dipped through the clouds, the body following until it was soaring within sight.

"There!" Tiffin yelled, pointing at the enemy. "There!" He had meant to communicate Rufus's location to the dragon, but in doing so, he had also ruined the element of surprise.

Rufus's chin tilted upward, and he held out a hand in the direction of the dragon.

In the same moment, a firebolt lanced through the sky, scorching a line across the darkness until it landed on the wicked etherae.

Tiffin cheered, throwing both fists in the air until the blaze died down. At its epicenter was a perfect circle of space unsinged or otherwise affected by the blast.

Rufus laughed again in a way that made Tiffin's horse stumble, and Tiffin was barely able to hold on. He apologized to his ride for yanking on its mane. The responding neigh forgave him, and they rode on, heading directly for their opponent.

Rufus's snarl was audible even at this distance, and he began throwing bolts of power at the dragon.

The stiguine altered its flight path, seemingly unbothered by the nuisance. He was circling lower now, and Tiffin felt the easy confidence narrowing his own vision. Rufus's outline was clear to him as though he were right in front of him. He realized he was seeing the man through the dragon's eyes.

They were close now, and Tiffin rode right to the wall. He had always admired its decorative pattern, but in the heat of battle, they suddenly looked different to him. The inset stones gave him a toe hold, and before long, he had scaled it all the way to the top.

The stiguine held the man's attention entirely. He was bent backwards, hurling insults and bindings at the beast and missing entirely.

Tiffin threw one aching leg over the edge and clambered up. He pulled his sword from its scabbard, ready to fight. He wasn't sure how, but he had to try. He studied his quarry, using the dragon's sight to find a point of weakness, but as the man drew the very lightning from the sky into his fingertips and channeled it upwards, Tiffin didn't see an opportunity.

From seemingly nowhere, twin spears of blue energy ripped through the air, wrapping themselves around Rufus.

Tiffin watched as it crackled around the etherae, his arms

and legs abruptly attached to his sides. He wriggled, but whether from pain or frustration, Tiffin couldn't determine.

The dragon was getting closer with every circle it made, and Tiffin held steady. Maybe he wouldn't need to attack. He followed the path of the ethereal ropes, finding Darius on the ground below. Both arms were outstretched, and his body was bowed forward under the effort.

Overhead, the stiguine screamed, circling the man, dropping blobs of burning saliva around him as it went.

The blue energy stopped, and Darius collapsed.

"NO!" Tiffin yelled, gripping the edge of the wall. There was nothing he could do for his mentor from here, and he turned back to Rufus.

The bindings that had been wrapped around Rufus disappeared. He yelled triumphantly, and his eyes landed on Tiffin.

"YOU!" Rufus yelled. "You got away once, but it won't happen again." He lifted one hand, summoning fire to his palm. The concentrated ball formed in an instant, and he launched it at Tiffin.

Instinctively, Tiffin rushed toward Rufus, dodging the tiny, lethal fireballs. One landed on his arm, and another hit his chest, but it was no more damaging than a fly. He burst forward, leading with his sword. He slashed when he was close enough, answered by the sickening sound of flesh parting around his blade.

Tiffin slipped on the wet stone, going down to his knees as he skidded several feet away.

The air whistled above him, and his sword fell from his hand. He clamped both hands over his ears and tumbled to a stop in the fetal position. He was facing Rufus now, his knees burning. He could see a trail of blood where his breeches had not survived the friction. He forced himself not to look at the damage to his flesh.

Face twisted with rage, Rufus yelled, "How dare—"

Whatever else Rufus was going to say was swallowed by the jaws of the stiguine snapping shut around his entire body.

Tiffin heard the crunch of bones as the dragon soared upwards, and delight rolled through his body. His belly was full and happy. He gasped in horror as he realized he was sharing the sensations of the dragon. He regurgitated in the back of his throat and squeezed his eyes shut.

Midday sun glared through his eyelids, turning the world red. He breathed, afraid to open his eyes or move or make a sound.

A wet splat caught his attention, and he peeked one eye open to see what had landed near him.

This time, Tiffin lost the contents of his stomach. The edges of his vision went dark, and he swayed on his feet. A disembodied human ear lay where it had plopped on the ground in front of him, like a discarded crumb. And everything went black.

The first thing Tiffin noticed when he regained consciousness was his mouth dry like ash and full of the coppery taste of blood. He smacked his tongue.

"Tiffin?"

The voice was soft and feminine, and he knew it immediately. It was Aunt Helen.

"Don't try to move, sweetheart. Don't even open your eyes. I'll get you some water," she promised.

He had no trouble obeying the instructions. He flexed his fingers, and immediately regretted it. He was suddenly aware of how scratchy the surface below him was and realized with a start that the palms of his hands were sticky with what he assumed was blood. There was a ringing in his ears, and it sounded like he was hearing the bustle of the room around him through water.

Before he could continue his self-assessment, a damp rag swiped over his forehead. It was soothing, and some of the tension he'd been holding in his jaw dissipated. He peeled one eye open to see the hand that was offering him succor. He blinked suddenly, both eyes wide in disbelief.

"Princess?" he mumbled.

Her soft smile was amused, and her dimple, the one he liked to study while she was having lessons, appeared on her cheek. Her flaxen locks swayed as she mopped his brow. What was she doing here?

"Calm yourself," she said, drawing her hand away.

He watched her dip the cloth into a nearby bowl and wring it out. Then she continued stroking it over his face. He frowned at the action, seeing the dark red stains on the cloth's surface. He wanted to say more, but his mouth was still too dry to formulate much.

"You're quite the hero," she announced, finally dropping the cloth in the bowl and folding her hands in her lap.

He arched a brow. At least that didn't hurt.

"I saw you from the window in the tower. I know I was supposed to be hiding, but after everyone was safe, I watched from the tower. The kitchen maids had it all under control and no one even knew I was gone." She snickered and covered it with her hand. "I'm clever like that."

"I knew," Aunt Helen announced as she returned with a

cup and sat on his opposite side. She leveled the girl with her gaze. "And if you ever do that again, I will kill you myself before the enemy has a chance."

The princess laughed louder at the remark. "I dare you to stop me. Besides, you're far too weak to hold me back now."

His aunt rolled her eyes and held out the cup she had brought. "Get me some water for this young man, please. I believe he's ready for it. I see the words all over his face," she teased.

Tiffin couldn't believe it when Princess Narette simply accepted the cup then turned to do as she was bidden. He wondered if his aunt had some innate talent for controlling people.

When they were alone, her voice lowered. "Be careful of that girl," she warned. "She's getting very headstrong. I never know what she is going to say or do next."

The princess returned with the cup of water, and Aunt Helen helped him lift his head to drink.

Water spilled over his mouth and down his neck as he tried. Helen pulled the cup away when he spluttered, and then the princess wiped away the rivulets on his neck.

"Slow down," Helen encouraged. "You'll be fine. Your knees will be on the mend for a while, so I'm afraid you'll have to stop your training until you've healed."

Tiffin took a dep breath and pulled himself into a sitting position. His hearing had improved as they conversed, and he looked at his legs for the first time. Each knee was wrapped in white cloth dotted with drying red circles across the top.

"It's a surface wound, but it was quite large," his aunt

explained. "The etherae treated the wounds. We'd like you to stay off your feet as much as you can for a few days. After that, moving around is the best thing for you."

Memories of the battle came rushing back to Tiffin, and he looked around. There had been so much lightning and power being wielded, and so much blood. He remembered Rufus being swallowed by the stiguine, and his stomach roiled in response.

His first words were almost inaudible as he mumbled. "What about Master Darius? Where is he? I saw him collapse."

Helen inclined her head to the bed a few feet to his right. "He's been in and out. The etherae say he needs rest after a battle as powerful as theirs." A proud smile curled her lips as she nodded at the princess. "I was standing behind her watching the whole thing. It was... impressive."

"You're welcome," the princess sassed with a giggle.

Helen rolled her eyes toward her royal charge. "At a time like this, you're going to tease me about a man?" she pressed.

The princess shrugged and directed her eyes to the ceiling. Her voice came out as a tuneless song. "You like him."

"I've said nothing of the sort. Master Darius is a well-respected etherae. An immensely powerful one too, if what his knight friends say holds any truth."

"But you do like him," the princess insisted. "In fact, I bet you even want to marry him." Her body shivered, her tongue dangling out of her mouth as she made a gagging noise. She glanced at the sleeping etherae. "You could do worse."

"Princess," Aunt Helen scolded. "Mind your tongue,

please."

The princess bit her lips together, seeming to cover a smile, but remained quiet as requested.

It wasn't until the evening of the following day that Darius regained consciousness. A hand bumped against Tiffin's where it dangled over the edge of his bed in the infirmary. He twisted to see the etherae reaching out to him.

"Master," he murmured. "Are you well? Let me get help."

Darius shook his head. "Be still, boy. I'm fine." His fingers gripped Tiffin's. "What happened?"

"The dragon ate Rufus," Tiffin blurted.

Darius blinked a few times before scrubbing one hand over his face and stretching. "Well, that settles matters quite neatly," he replied.

Tiffin chuckled, but it faded after a moment. "If it wasn't for the stiguine, it looked like Rufus would have beaten you."

Darius did not answer.

"Is he stronger than you? I mean, was he?"

"I suppose that depends on how you define strength. He was angry on a level that I have never experienced." He went quiet.

"So, anger made him stronger?" Tiffin pressed. He had plenty of anger, but he didn't believe that was what fueled the etherae he knew.

"Emotions certainly influence the power you can draw at any given moment. But it's unsafe for extended periods of time."

"In our training, you have always encouraged me to free my mind."

He nodded. "Infusing passion into a skill before you

have mastered it is dangerous. Like adding oil to a fire. In my worst moment, I have never felt it run that deeply. And he fostered that anger for at least fifteen years before attacking."

"I can't believe he was willing to take out so many villagers to get back at you."

"Always keep counsel nearby. They will keep you on the true path." Darius sighed heavily and stretched again.

Their conversation was interrupted as his aunt breezed in.

"I thought I heard your voice," Helen pronounced as she joined them. "Voices," she corrected, looking between Tiffin and Darius. "I'm having food brought for you."

"Helen," Darius murmured, and his lips quirking into a smile.

Tiffin watched as he stared at her, his blue eyes intense and unwavering. With revolting recognition, he noticed Helen staring back...as though Tiffin wasn't there at all. Even worse, she placed her fingers on his forearm. Tiffin thought he might be sick.

When the etherae reached for her hand to pull it into his own, Tiffin excused himself to see what was taking so long with the food.

He wound his way slowly through the corridors. The skin on his knees was beginning to recover, and they had removed the disgusting smelling poultices as long as he promised not to go falling on his knees again any time soon.

The noise of pots and pans and waft of steam rising through the stairwell were comforting, and he sniffed the air in an attempt to guess what treat would be waiting for him. What he had not expected was the sight of his father backed against the countertops as Myra held a spoon to his lips.

"Go on. You'll like it. I'm an amazing cook," she insisted.

He watched as his father obliged, lips puckered as he sucked in the broth.

Myra pulled back with a smile, turning her cheeks into apples. "Good, isn't it?" she hummed.

His father relaxed as he savored the sample in his mouth and nodded. "Yes. Very good."

Sensing his father needed to be rescued, Tiffin intervened. "Dad," he called.

Aaron jumped at the word and turned to face him. "Tiff!" he called, scuttling toward him. "Should you be up and around?"

Tiffin shrugged. "I heard that food was coming up for Master Darius. He's awake."

"Oh yes, right!" Myra began gathering items onto a tray and barking orders at the other kitchen helpers. "Heavens, I don't know what kept me."

Tiffin thought he had seen exactly where her focus was, and he studied Myra in a different light. She was his favorite person in the kitchen, and he loved her food, but she was far too aggressive for his father, and she would make his dad fat.

"He's awake?" Aaron repeated. "Good. I want to give him a piece of my mind for letting you go on that fool's mission to save him!" Aaron barged past Tiffin, taking the stairs out of the kitchen two at a time.

Given his current situation, Tiffin thought it quite rude to have run away. He hobbled up the steps past his father, wishing he was still wearing his dragon armor as blocked his father's path. "Stop, Dad. Please." He placed a hand on his father's barrel chest.

Aaron paused. "You're my only son."

"I know, Dad. But he didn't ask me to do this or tell me to. In fact, he always tells me to hide when there is danger. Don't be mad at me for protecting the people I care about the way you raised me to do."

A grimace crossed his father's face. "You don't have to go acting like an adult all of a sudden because you saved the day," he groused.

Chapter 15

A fortnight later, Aaron was smoothing out Tiffin's hair. Tiffin pushed his father's hand away. "Stop, Dad. You're making it worse."

Aaron's hands drew back defensively. "Sorry. Trying to help."

Sighing, he nodded. "I know. Thank you." Tiffin straightened his collar beneath the heavy emerald robe settled across his shoulders. He wasn't used to his father seeming skittish, but as they stood in the antechamber facing a pair of large double doors, it was the sole word that came to mind. It reminded him of one of their goats when strange horses were nearby.

At any moment, the doors were going to open, and he and his father would be heralded inside. And they would meet the king.

Tiffin often forgot how privileged he was to know the princess and so many of the castle staff. But the remainder of the royal family had always remained a mystery. Until now. Today there would be a gathering of unearthly proportions, and part of his mind worried about assembling so many powerful individuals in one place.

Before his brain could be consumed by worry, the doors parted, and the sound of harps wafted into the space around him. A royal page waited at the opening of the doors, nodding first to Tiffin and then to his father.

Squaring his shoulders, Tiffin moved forward, his father a pace behind him on the left. His feet skimmed across the runner indicating the aisle. He had been instructed to look forward and not gawk like he wanted, but the room full of hooded etherae made it difficult. Their cloaks varied in color, denoting their status. He passed the green cloaks first, then the blue, the purple, and the gold until he reached the dais. In front of him stood Darius, outfitted in a silvery white robe. Behind him were the king and queen, and Tiffin's step hitched slightly at the sight of Princess Narette to their right. His aunt was standing proudly behind her, and she inclined her head ever so slightly as she cast him a grin.

At Tiffin's approach, Darius pushed his hood back. The fabric pooled around his shoulders, and his well-trimmed goatee emphasized his stern expression.

Tiffin's spine stiffened at the sight, and his mouth went dry.

Darius's baritone filled the hall with precise, reverent tones. "Your majesties, King Daniel and Queen Martha, I present to you Tiffin Vanheusen, son of Aaron Vanheusen, blacksmith to His Royal Majesty."

Dropping to his knees in a bow, Tiffin looked at the toe of his shoe. He saw his father's shadow dropping behind him. The heavy fabric robe was hot enveloping his body, and he wasn't clear on how long he should assume this stance and waited for permission to stand. To his surprise, he heard footsteps approaching.

"Rise, Tiffin Vanheusen, hero, and you also, Aaron Vanheusen, blacksmith by trade and father to a hero." The king's words rolled slowly around the room.

Tiffin's legs shook as he lifted himself to his feet, eyes remaining on the floor. He willed his breathing to remain controlled.

"We gather today to honor this boy and his family for their bravery in times of crisis within this kingdom and neighboring realms. When asked to find a scale from the dragon besieging our lands, this boy rode out to save us in the night, with a horse, a sword, and chain mail. Not only did he succeed in his quest, but he also rescued three of our knights and Grand Master Darius in the process and liberated a stiguine dragon from imprisonment. Not to mention that during the recent battle, Tiffin Vanheusen put himself in harm's way between the princess and our foe with no thought to his own safety."

The king's steps wandered closer, and Tiffin wondered where he was going until he stopped before Aaron.

"Aaron Vanheusen, show me your countenance."

Tiffin desperately wanted to look over his shoulder to witness what was about to happen.

"For your expert smithery and your wisdom in raising your son to sacrifice his own safety for that of the kingdom, I wish to honor you with a gift. Your faithful service to the crown has not gone unnoticed. With gratitude, I name you vassal of the southern lands in which you and your family have worked for many decades."

The page who had led Tiffin into the room scurried to the king's side with a scroll. He heard his father sniffling and turned his gaze on his aunt. Helen's mouth gaped. A second later, her lips closed, and her eyes turned to the back wall. She placed one hand on Narette's shoulder, her posture like a statue.

"Thank you, Your Majesty," Aaron mumbled, his voice shaky.

The king's wanderings continued until he stopped in front of Tiffin. He reached a knuckle to Tiffin's chin, lifting it slightly. "Your bravery is unparalleled. I have heard many retellings of your adventures, of your valor in the face of tasks much larger than you, and your selfless heroism toward my daughter. You have fought at the sides of my most courageous knights, and the esteemed Grand Master Etherae Darius. Without you, the creeping sickness would be upon us all. I have been told that your greatest wish is to train at the academy to join these etherae surrounding us. Is this true?"

Tiffin started to nod, but remembered that his answers must be verbal, and he cleared his throat. "Yes, sir," he replied, his eyes meeting the king's.

"And it is my understanding that your training will be guided by my very own Master Darius." At this, the king gripped Darius's shoulder.

"That is correct, Your Majesty," Darius affirmed. His eyes roamed from the king, to Tiffin, and then to the crowd behind them. "Tiffin is a dedicated pupil with untapped, and I believe vast potential. It is my desire for him to become my apprentice."

"Very well," the king approved. "From this day forward, Tiffin Vanheusen, you will be known as Apprentice to the Royal Grand Master Etherae Darius. And as meager thanks for your service to the crown, your tutelage shall be sponsored by the crown. You shall be given quarters next to your liege in the castle and shall be granted full access to the kingdom. As part of your sponsorship, staff will be provided to your family's land. Upon completion of your training, you will become a member of the royal etherae, bound to serve and protect us with the knowledge we have given you. Do you accept?"

Tiffin had known he was going to be allowed to study—Darius had confirmed this days ago, and they had already begun training. There was already one villager managing their household chores, and Myra had already started sending baskets of food. He had not expected to have a patron. He wanted to dance and scream and shake everyone in the room to share the good news. Instead, he inclined his head toward the king.

"I do."

"Then kneel, Tiffin Vanheusen," Darius instructed. His lips held the barest hint of a smile.

Smoothly, Tiffin dropped to one knee, bowing before his master.

Darius produced an ornate gold scepter from inside his robe, extending it toward Tiffin. Its bejeweled tip tapped first on his left shoulder, then his right, and then rested gently on the top of his head.

"I name thee my apprentice. I vow to guide and train you in the ways of the etherae and impart to you their sacred knowledge and wisdom. As my apprentice, you will be afforded my protection, mind and body, from those that would seek to harm you or your reputation.

"As my apprentice, you shall, in return, dedicate your

whole self toward the pursuit of knowledge and skill to fulfill your potential and accept my instruction without quarrel. Rise, Apprentice Tiffin, son of Aaron and Hero of the Kingdom."

Tears escaped the corners of Tiffin's eyes as he rose. The weight of someone's gaze made him squirm, and he searched the dais for the culprit, expecting it to be his aunt. Instead, the princess stared unabashedly, a dimple on each cheek, just for him.

Every etherae in the room stood for him, and the king's brash clapping spread throughout the room. Darius turned him bodily to face his brothers and sisters of the craft, squeezing his shoulders gently in congratulations. The master's words were hot near his ear, and Tiffin strained to hear him over the applause.

"Welcome, brother."

For the first time, he noticed Pierce, Kaiden, and Elias in the front row, their uniforms strange and formal, setting them apart from the other robed figures. Smiles lit each of their faces without remorse as they cheered. In unison, the three held a fist over their hearts and nodded at him. Tiffin returned the gesture, then bowed to everyone.

When he lifted his head again, Tiffin stared into the faces of his new family. He had never imagined he would do anything more than tend goats and horses. But maybe that's what happened when he meddled with dragons—his whole life was about to soar.

The End

ABOUT THE AUTHOR

Laura Christian was raised in St. Louis, MO but now resides in the great state of Texas with her husband, a Russian Blue cat, a Siamese cat, and a Jack Russel Terrier. In her spare time, Laura enjoys reading, sewing, knitting, painting, and mostly playing Fortnite with her besties.

To learn more about the author and other publications, please visit www.thelaurachristian.com for more details.